DANCING WITH DOUBT

BARRE TO BAR
BOOK THREE

SUMMER COOPER

LOVY BOOKS

Lovy Books Ltd
20-22 Wenlock Road
London N1 7GU

Cover by SC Creative

Roxie

"June, oh, uh..." Roxie looked around the front porch of Lincoln's home and tried to find somewhere to hide. There was nothing to lurch behind, so she stood there, clutching the panels of her dress together. "Hi."

"Is it really you?" June stepped out of the house to pull Roxie into a hug, but Roxie found a place, at last, to take refuge at the bottom of the steps. June looked hurt, confused, as she began to speak again. "Where have you been all this time? I can't believe it."

With a swipe of her hands, Roxie managed to button up the dress she'd unbuttoned earlier. June didn't need to see her boobs, even if Roxie had been proud to have those boobs since the day she'd bought them. "How are you, June? It's been a while."

Roxie's thoughts ran through a dozen answers as June gaped at her, standing there like a fish gasping for air. Roxie had dressed in a manner to seduce Lincoln. He'd written that he needed her in the text message. She'd come to his place ready for seduction, dressed in an empire-waisted babydoll, the tiniest pair of panties she had, more strings than anything, and the garters and stockings she knew he loved. On top of it, she'd worn a black coat dress and some heels. Not exactly the attire she'd have chosen to meet her childhood friend in. She thought this kind of scene would only happen in fiction, a movie or something, but nope, the total humiliation of being met by the last person she expected to meet had really happened.

Roxie's hair, newly dyed a dark purple and black, curled with a silky, glossy shine around her head. The hair, makeup, and outfit should have disguised her against anyone that didn't know her, yet here June was, pulling her old name out of thin air as if she were still that blonde kid with no boobs, dressed in jeans and a hoodie, pining over June's brother Liam. Instead, that girl now answered to Roxie and did a whole hell of a lot more than pine for Lincoln, June's other brother.

"Holy fucking moly, I can't believe this is happening," Roxie muttered as she drew her hands up to her face and side-eyed June. Why hadn't he warned her his sister would be here? "Uh, hi June. Um, can we go inside? Talk maybe?"

Her words came out short and sweet because she didn't actually want to go in at all. She'd often wondered what had become of June and had even looked her up online to satisfy her curiosity, but she hadn't wanted to answer the questions that would come from reconnecting with the girl who was now a fully-grown woman. And a doctor, according to her LinkedIn profile.

June bit her lip. Her brown eyes, a mirror of her half-Chinese mother's, pinched with concern. She held her right hand out to Roxie and seemed to relax when the other woman took it. Roxie wasn't so relaxed, she was more on guard than ever, but she knew she had to face this moment. June would not let her leave without an explanation.

They walked into the house, hand in hand for the first time since that long-ago day when Roxie's life had changed completely. Roxie tried not to remember the last time she saw June, it only brought her pain, and focused instead on how nice it was to be around the one person who'd always made her feel whole.

"So, Lolly, how have you been?" June asked once they were in the kitchen and coffee was brewing. Her pale skin paled even more when Roxie winced. "Did I say something wrong?"

"No, it's just, well..." Roxie paused, trying to think of how to explain it, "I don't really go by Chloe anymore. I'm Roxie now."

"Oh." June chirped, her eyes going wide. "I, uh, that's an interesting name."

"A stripper's name you mean?" Roxie smiled, letting her friend off the hook. "Yeah, that's kind of why I chose it."

"Ah, I see." June's knitted eyebrows proved she didn't quite see, not really.

"I'm an exotic dancer. Pole dancer, whatever you want to call it. I even teach classes and do charity events, so it's not all bad." Roxie's eyebrows went up and she pulled her lips in to try to smother her laughter.

"Ohhhh!" June exclaimed in a loud rush, her left palm coming up to gently slap her forehead. "Damn, I can be so dense sometimes."

"It's okay. You probably weren't expecting me to do that kind of dancing." Roxie got up and prepared two mugs of coffee, asking over her shoulder if June still took hers the same way she had when they were teenagers.

"Yeah, I do. Not much has changed about me since I last saw you." June shrugged and her cheeks turned bright pink.

"Nothing wrong with that. And you are a doctor now." Roxie brought the white mugs over to the table before she sat down across from June at the table. "I'd say a lot has changed about you."

June's smile bloomed to life, her perfectly straight, pearly white teeth a testament to her dentist. "I'm in town for a medical conference for fertility doctors or I wouldn't be here now. So, yeah, I guess a lot has changed."

"The girl I used to know didn't want to travel at all. You said you'd had enough of it over the years." Roxie tried to keep the conversation off of herself and on June instead. She didn't want to explain anything, not if she could help it. The conversation was inevitable, surely, but Roxie wanted to put it off as long as she could.

"Why did you disappear?" June asked when Roxie had expected her to explain why she didn't mind traveling now. The unexpected turn made Roxie blink.

"There was the fire." She answered hesitantly, her face scrunched in a frown. "It scared me and, well, I just wasn't thinking straight, I guess."

Her answer, accompanied with a shrug, didn't seem to appease June at all. "You weren't the kind to run away, Lol-I mean Roxie. And you know I'd have helped you do anything you needed me to."

"I know, there was some trouble that nobody could help me with, though. Stuff to do with my parents and things I didn't know about until after the fire." Roxie sat back in her chair, trying to get away from June's penetrating stare that was so like Lincoln's, even if they did have different fathers. Roxie suspected that look was in their DNA.

"I still could have helped you." June protested, frowning at Roxie with annoyance now, the confusion long gone. "I would have helped you hide bodies, or run away, or whatever it was you needed me to do. I worried about you for so long, I nearly made myself sick. Lincoln finally told me he knew where you were and that you were fine, just so I would eat again."

Roxie's heart squeezed at the way her friend had worried for her and she reached across the table to grab June's hand. "I didn't mean to worry you or ghost you, it's just what happened. I had a lot on my plate then."

"I wish Lincoln would have told me more. He never told me where you were, why you'd left, or anything like that, and after that one time, he didn't speak about you again. I always wondered why but you know how he is, you can't get answers out of him if he's determined to keep his mouth shut."

"I know." Roxie gave a rueful smile but deep down she was touched that he'd kept her secrets, even if he had revealed to June that he knew she was safe. She could understand that and knew he hadn't given anything away, or else June would have found her long ago.

"So, all the trouble is gone now?" June asked, her eyebrows higher on her forehead.

"Yeah." Roxie nodded, but she didn't quite meet June's gaze. "Seems so."

"Good, then we can catch up and spend time together again." June giggled, a sound that Roxie remembered from their childhood and suddenly, she was that carefree girl she used to be, if only for the moment.

"God, I've missed you." She let June's hand go and sat back in the chair to cross her legs under the table. "Life just hasn't been the same without you."

"Or you." June quickly replied, sipping at her coffee. She pointed at Roxie with her mug. "You don't know what it was like comparing other girls to you when I started at the university. It wasn't so bad at med school, I didn't have time to talk to anyone, barely even my family."

"I'm irreplaceable, huh?" Roxie teased, but June nodded somberly.

"You are, you really are." June's soft smile was back, and it was her eyes that wandered now, avoiding Roxie's blue gaze. "I was never really good at making friends, but it never mattered when you were there with me."

"You had plenty of other friends." Roxie protested,

remembering all the girls that used to flock around them. They'd only ever really needed each other back then but other girls were always around.

"Not really, they were all attracted to you, like moths to flames," June answered poetically and that made them both laugh unexpectedly. "Good grief, that was bad."

"No, but it was close." Roxie teased and just like that, they were old friends again, completely at ease. Or, as at ease as Roxie could manage these days. "I hadn't planned on meeting you again, not in this lifetime, but I'm glad I did."

"Speaking of, how long have you and Lincoln been dating?" June asked nonchalantly, but the way she tilted her head made that a lie.

"We aren't." Roxie corrected her quickly, putting that idea to bed. "We're just…friends."

"Mmhmm, I don't believe you for some reason." June glanced down at the dress that Roxie thought she'd closed surreptitiously earlier and knew June had caught the move. "Or is this your every day, going to see a friend look?"

"Really, ask Lincoln. We're just friends." Roxie wanted to be honest with her friend and explain the current situation between her and Lincoln, but he was a private person, he wouldn't appreciate her spilling the beans. Add to that the fact that she'd become rather closed off herself over the last ten years, and, well, opening up to anyone but Lincoln was hard. Their contract was up and neither had talked about renewing it since they'd come back from Cambodia. Explaining that to June was just not something she was willing to do.

"I'll buy it, for now," June said with narrowed eyes, clearly not buying any of it. "I can respect your need for privacy though. I haven't told my parents how much I hate being a doctor, so I can understand not wanting to talk about Lincoln. Even if you won't explain to me why you'd be friends with Lincoln and not reconnect with me immediately."

Roxie noted the hurt in June's voice but chose to focus on the other thing she'd said. "You hate being a doctor?"

"Well, kind of, yes and no. I love helping people have children, that part is great. It's the constant tremendous stress I'm under and knowing a patient's life is in my hands when I'm performing procedures that really gets to me. I hate those parts. And the constant disappointment for some patients, even when I warn them that they aren't good candidates for some of the treatments they want. It's heartbreaking and sometimes, I just want to disappear and start a new life."

"I can understand that." Roxie's head bent down as shame flooded through her. The unspoken 'like you did' stung. She knew June didn't mean it that way, but the implication was still there. "I can even recommend it in some respects, but in others? You end up missing people and parts of your old life. And you have to change, become someone new and that isn't always a good thing."

"I can promise you, giving up my life in New York wouldn't be such a bad thing." June laughed softly and picked up her mug, sipping at the coffee before she spoke again. "I could devote more time to drawing my Japanese Zen circles, which is something I do before every surgery or procedure. It lets me know if I'm in a good mental state before each procedure and helps me to focus. If my hands are too shaky to draw, I take a minute, practice some breathing exercises, stuff like that."

"You're under a lot of pressure, aren't you?" Roxie asked, her concern thick in her voice.

"Yeah, I'm the head of the fertility department at Dad's medical group. The Bennet Medical Group owns the hospital, an online clinic that operates through apps, a pharmacy, several fertility clinics, vision correction clinics in Europe, and probably more places I can't remember at the moment. There's too much to remember." June gave a shy smile before she shrugged. "Anyway, I have to get ready to go to this conference but maybe we can meet up again, before I go back to New York?"

"Sure, yeah, give me your phone, I'll give you my number," Roxie said and took June's phone. "I've added my email too, if you want to use that instead."

"Cool. I'm glad I found you again, Lol-I mean Roxie." June's wide smile was back again, her face which had barely changed in the last ten years was as familiar to Roxie as her own.

"I'm glad you did, too, even if it was by accident," Roxie said, thinking over all the things she'd left unsaid, or deliberately avoided saying. Like how it was Lincoln who'd helped her escape from those men that night, and why it was important for her to keep a lot of things to herself now.

Years ago, she'd have poured everything out to June, but now? Now, there were secrets she had to keep from everybody, even herself in some regards. Things she would not allow herself to think about, except for those nights when she was totally alone, unable to fight off her guilty conscience.

"I hate to break this up, but I have to give a speech. Otherwise, I'd blow it off." June said apologetically but Roxie waved her off.

"It's not a problem. We'll meet up again soon. I promise." Roxie hoped she could keep that promise. "I'd better find Lincoln anyway and find out what he was after."

"But you aren't dating at all. Mmhmm." June pulled

her bottom lip in, but it did nothing to hide her grin or the impish light in her eyes.

"We aren't." Roxie laughed with her friend, but she wasn't actually telling a fib, was she? After all, contracts weren't for those that were romantically involved, were they?

2

Lincoln

He'd left his house as soon as he'd shown June to an unused bedroom. Her showing up on his doorstep was a surprise, but it shouldn't have been. His family often treated each other's homes like hotels, his especially. June showing up shouldn't have been a surprise at all, even if he couldn't remember if he'd told his mother that he'd bought a place in South Carolina. Not that his mother couldn't get the information she wanted out of either of his PAs. His mother was adept at that.

His frustration levels had been through the roof when he texted Roxie, telling her he needed her. Now? He could rattle his sister's head around in a box for interrupting what he'd hoped would be one very hot night of sex with Roxie. Damn it all.

He drove around town for an hour, trying to find something to do, some way of keeping his mind off of his sister, his frustration, and Roxie. Maybe it was fate that had a hand in June showing up? It would keep him away from Roxie for a little while longer. Not that he couldn't meet her at her hotel, but the interruption was a very good reminder that ending things with her was for the best.

A flash on the center computer panel and a chime that interrupted the music let him know someone was calling him. A quick glance at the dash told him it was Tanya, his stealthy super-secret spy PA. He ended up pulling over at a shopping plaza to take the call from Tanya and ask her how things were going over at Roxie's apartment.

"It's quiet, *Mr. Young.*" Tanya immediately put him on edge by addressing him as Mr. Young and stressing his last name. It was something she insisted on doing, even when she saw it made him cringe. Bitch.

"No signs of any of the assholes we're tracking?" Lincoln asked, his brown eyes on the window of a lingerie shop, but he didn't really see the skimpy attire. He was back in boss mode.

"Not a whiff of them, boss. I think it might be safe for her to come back." Tanya answered, sounding bored and annoyed. But then she would be, she wanted Lincoln for herself. She didn't want him taking care of some beautiful exotic dancer like Roxie. Tanya would never say it, but she'd make her thoughts clear at every turn.

"I'll drop by, see what improvements we can make to her security. Are those men Kai arranged to have surveil the place around?" He put the car in gear and headed for a drive-through restaurant at the end of the plaza.

"Yeah, they're here, want to talk to one of them?" Tanya asked, still sounding annoyed.

"Yes, I would." He sighed, let his own annoyance come through in the words. "Can you pretend to not be such a bitch, Tanya?"

"What?" She asked innocently, though they both knew it was contrived. "Do I not sound pleased that I've spent weeks staring at an empty apartment, taking turns with other people that sit and stare at the same place? I mean, what could be better? What could make use of my skills more than this?"

"Stop complaining, I'm paying you triple to sit there and eat burgers and drink milk shakes. Speaking of, do you want anything while I'm ordering?" Lincoln already knew she'd say yes.

"Yeah, I'll take one of those weird footlong chili dogs with coleslaw on it. I don't know why I like them, but I do. And a pineapple milkshake, please, if they have them." She replied before she told him she was with the man he'd asked to speak to.

"What's up, Mr. Young?" A man asked in a monotone voice. That must be Petey, then. The man never seemed to have the energy to muster anything more than a monotone voice, but then, he was well over six-feet tall and lanky as hell. He probably had no energy to speak of.

"Just checking in, Petey. How's it going?" Lincoln drove up to the window and waited for Petey to finish before he placed his order. The other man repeated what Tanya had said, almost word for word, so Lincoln ended the call after he'd acknowledged the man's report and told him he'd be there soon.

When he drove up to the street Roxie lived on, he noted that everything was quiet except for the dry cleaner's which seemed to be doing a booming business. "What's the deal with that place?"

Tanya turned to him as he slid into her car and gave a devilish grin. "Oh, I think there's a little more than dry cleaning going on, Mr. Young. Got my hot dog?"

Lincoln handed her the bag and she passed him the small version of the giant hot dog she'd asked for. "I ordered some curly fries for you too. I know you like those."

"Thanks." She answered and popped a fry into her mouth.

"So, what kind of business are we talking then?" Lincoln unwrapped his hot dog and started to munch on it, loving the concoction despite his usually healthy routine. Tanya had introduced him to the treat and neither had been able to go a week without one. He'd do extra laps later, to burn it off.

"I can't make up my mind. I've seen bums walk in there, and come out with food, and I've seen businessmen go in and come out with a donut box. It's always something different. I don't know if it's drugs, money laundering, or what. Maybe it's a combo. Or maybe clients like their dry cleaning covered in chocolate icing, I don't know." Tanya shrugged, her pretty face friendly but not as full of adoration as it usually was.

That was a relief to Lincoln, but he frowned as a thought occurred to him. "Should you be eating that much salt with your kidney problems?"

"No, not at all, but sometimes you have to make sacrifices. I'll probably hate myself for it later, but right now, this hot dog wins out against my willpower. I'll catch hell when I go in for dialysis, so I'll have to find some soon."

"I'll stop buying you junk food then. How's your daughter?" He asked, watching the door to the dry cleaners open. A woman came out carrying a dazzling ruby-red, sequin-covered box. Must be a special dress, he decided and balled up the food wrapper after he took the last bite.

"She's fine," Tanya said after a pause. She'd nearly finished the hot dog that was twice as big as his and took another bite without going into detail.

Well, wasn't this just a party? He thought as he noticed the security team Kai sent, hiding in a black van with a logo for a communications company that he knew was fake. That logo would come off and be replaced with a furniture store logo tomorrow, or maybe one for a plumber. There must have been quite a few logos stored in a hidden panel of the van. Maybe he should go talk to the guys there.

"They know any more than you do?" Lincoln nudged his chin in the direction of the van.

"I doubt it, those bozos are all about listening, not watching. They've heard a lot of stuff that sounds like it might be code to me, but they seem to think it's normal to ask for a dozen creams at a dry cleaner's place. They could be right, creams could be cream cleaners or something. Who knows?"

"If you're bored, Tanya, I can find somebody else to do this. They're our ears, you're our eyes." He reminded her and frowned in her direction. He caught the way she rolled her eyes before she looked at him.

"It's fine. I'm just not used to this humidity. Or sitting around for hours doing nothing."

"I know, but I'm glad you're here. I know I can trust you." He replied, nodding his head.

"You can. And I meant it, you know? I don't think anyone is coming back here. And with that Wendy woman always keeping an eye out, I think Roxie'll be safe. Plus, you can always get Kai to send more security over if you're still worried."

"You could be right." He sighed and slouched in the seat that was almost too small for him. It had been a long day and he still wanted to see Roxie. Even more now that he was at the place that had been her home for so long.

"You going to bring her back, then?" Tanya pushed for an answer, not looking at him, but at the building to their left, across the street.

"I might. I'm not sure yet." He swiped at his face with his left hand, not sure what to do. Roxie was probably pissed at him for not being at his house.

Which would be totally understandable, he admitted to himself, he had sent her a text guaranteed to bring her to him. And had run when his sister showed up before she did. What made matters worse was he knew Roxie didn't want to meet anyone from her old life, especially anyone from his family. She hadn't spoken to June on purpose, he'd known that all these years.

That's why he'd told June that Chloe was fine all those years ago and hadn't mentioned meeting her as

Roxie ten years later. Whether it was to keep June safe or to keep her identity secret, or both, didn't matter. He should have known leaving her to meet June on his doorstep had been a shitty thing to do.

Fuck, fuck, fuck - everything was a mess really, when he thought about it. He shouldn't have started the affair with Roxie, even if it had come in the form of a contract. He should have made sure she was safe, kept her at arm's length, and moved on. But here he was, sitting in his PA's shitty car, watching Roxie's apartment for any number of men that might be after her for a variety of reasons that went from an ex-boyfriend who owed the wrong people money, to whatever shit it was her father had become embroiled in a decade ago.

"Did I tell you we got some more info about the Abshires?" Tanya asked just as he was about to shove himself out of the car.

"What?" His head whipped around, and he relaxed. "What new info?"

"Yeah, I don't know why it didn't show up all those years ago, but we've just found out that Mr. Abshire, Chloe's dad, booked three tickets to Paris right before the fire. Chloe wanted to go abroad to study ballet, didn't she? Well, she got into the school in Paris, and it seems Daddy Dearest rented an apartment for them all there."

"So they were going to leave town, but that didn't

happen. Interesting." He was about to lose himself in thinking when Tanya spoke up again.

"And then there's Mr. Abshire's sister that we didn't know about." She said quietly, as if dropping a bomb, because of course, she was.

"What sister?" Lincoln shot back, confused.

"Exactly. A sister we didn't know about. She has a number in Paris that the PI tracked down."

"Weird. How did we not know any of this?" Lincoln swiped his face again before he looked at Tanya.

"She's not listed as an Abshire, she's got a different last name, Chedotal. As for the rest, it seems there are two police files on the Abshires. One that was released to the public and another one from an investigator who died under mysterious circumstances. The PI just got his hands on those files."

"Damn, damn, damn. What a mess. All of that would have been helpful to know back then. It would have changed everything for Chloe." Lincoln said, realizing his mistake immediately. She wasn't Chloe anymore and never would be if he'd come to know anything about her. "What else did the file say?"

"That the Abshires were shot and that's how they died, not from smoke inhalation as the other reports claim."

Now that was a bomb. Fuck.

"Why am I not surprised?" Lincoln exhaled, feeling exhausted suddenly.

"Because we know better?" Tanya said as an answer. "I think this stinks of the mafia, or some other gang activity. I'm guessing Mr. Abshire wasn't the type for gang activity though, was he?"

"No, he wasn't. Definitely not. But the mob? He might have got on their wrong side by accident." Lincoln turned his head to stare out at the empty street and watched a stray flyer spin by. The streets weren't typically dirty there, but on days when flyers went out you would see one or two blowing along a street. Miles better than any day in New York City, even with the street sweepers out.

"What do you want me to do?" Tanya asked, moving around to get more comfortable.

"Nothing, for now. I've got to get all this straight in my head." Guilt ate at him because he still hadn't told Roxie about any of this. He knew he should have told her, but he wasn't even sure who it was that had gone after her and her family ten years ago. What could he explain? Oh, hey Rox, I know your parents died and some guys scared the shit out of you so you ran, but guess what? You've inherited some money? Oh, and your parents were shot.

That would probably break her.

He didn't want to break her, he wanted to make her

life make sense, make it so she didn't have to hide anymore. The more time that passed, he found himself wanting to be a part of the future she deserved, but watching his mother had taught him true love didn't last. Even dollar signs couldn't keep his mother happy in the end, which was why she'd hopped from marriage to marriage.

Okay, Roxie wasn't like that, but would this need they had for each other last?

He couldn't guarantee that, and even if he'd started to want more from her, that didn't mean they'd even still like each other in fifteen years. Maybe even less time, if he went by his mother's track record. Even his siblings hadn't settled down yet.

Damn, this was not his night, he thought and sat up straight. "I'm going to get out of here. Stick around until your relief comes. I'd like to keep eyes on this place for a while longer, even if she comes back. Especially if she comes back, actually."

"Sure thing, Mr. Young." Tanya saluted and gave him a wink.

"Bitch." He muttered as he got out of Tanya's car and headed for his own. Now, if he could put Roxie in her place as easily as he did Tanya, his life would be so much easier. Something told him that would never, ever happen. Still, the thought made him smile.

3

Lincoln

He'd let too much go by the wayside since Chloe came back into his life as Roxie. He'd been fascinated by the life she'd built for herself, had wanted to know every aspect of the life she'd chosen to live since she'd left him alone in a hotel all those years ago. He'd got caught up in her, in sex with her, in enjoying her, and he'd let the past fall away. Reality had taken a backseat, but it was time to stop that.

He got back into his car but sent a text without starting the engine. There was no need to start it when he'd just asked Roxie to meet him at her apartment.

He settled into the car to wait for her, putting the AC on to fight off some of the heat outside. It wasn't as bad as it could be in Cambodia, but it was starting to get miserable in the car. He also knew there'd be hell to pay when Roxie did show up, if she did.

Springing June on her, well, leaving her to come face to face with June, hadn't been his brightest idea or his most shining moment. He regretted doing it now, but he'd been thrown by his half-sister's presence and had reacted badly. He'd wanted privacy down here, to be who he wanted to be while he investigated what was going on with Chloe/Roxie, but yet again, his family intruded.

That really pissed him off, but it wasn't June's fault. They'd all done the same thing to each other for years, and it was only now that he wanted his privacy that the way they all passed like ships in the night, docking in each other's berths, made him resent the behavior. She wasn't to know, because he hadn't said anything to anybody.

His phone chirped and Lincoln grimaced because it was the tune he'd assigned to Roxie. How had she responded? He'd hoped she'd just show up here, smiling, and would forgive him for dropping his sister on her.

Fuck you, Lincoln. He saw her words through another grimace, one eye closed.

Fuck, she was pissed.

She had a right to be, but they had shit to deal with, like ending the relationship they had and getting it back to something he could handle. Or taking it to a different level that he could handle. A platonic level.

But even a text saying 'fuck you' made him think of her in ways that were definitely not platonic.

He didn't respond to the text, he just waited to see if she showed up. When he saw her car, he got out of his own and headed across the street to meet her.

"Why am I here?" She asked as soon as she got out of the car. He noted the dress she had on, the heels, and suspected the black hose wasn't hose, but stockings with a delightful little garter belt cinched around her waist. Oh, that outfit hurt, and it hurt a lot.

"Because we need to talk about a few things. Let's go inside, shall we?" He directed but she stood her ground.

"Explain to me exactly why I should agree to let you into my apartment?" The keyring in her hand, heavily burdened with a rainbow of colored keys jangled in her hand as she crossed her arms over her breasts, her left eyebrow up.

Yep, she was still pissed.

"Because we're two adults that have shit to talk about and the street isn't the place to do it." He answered and took her elbow to guide her up the stairs to her door. She allowed him to do that, but he could feel her gaze burning into his head from the side.

Super-pissed.

Damn.

"You planned this, didn't you?" She said the moment she had the door open and had walked inside. She didn't seem to notice that she had new furniture or that Wendy had made good on her promise to put every-thing back together. It was as neat and tidy as it had been before her ex took a hammer and knife to it all. And probably a screwdriver too.

"Planned what, Roxie?" He asked, thinking that she was accusing him of fixing her apartment. She was right, of course, he'd paid for the new furniture and every-thing Wendy needed to make repairs to the place. But why would she spit that at him?

"June, you giant asshole. Your *sister*! You set me up to meet with her." Roxie walked over to the new couch made from a red velvety material, but then went back to the kitchen area to pace. "You knew I'd say no and decided you knew what was best for me, right? Because you always seem to think you know what's best for me when I can guarantee you, you don't, Lincoln."

Her face was stony with anger, her eyes hard and cold with suppressed rage. Her cover was blown and he knew she was entitled to every bit of rage she felt, but it wasn't his fault. Well, not really.

"Look, you really need to stop running from the truth, Roxie. There are things you don't know." He was about to tell her the things he'd learned today, but she barked out a harsh laugh and smirked at him.

"Right, things that I should know but you've only just now decided to tell me, am I right? Because, yet again, you fucking know better than me. Just fuck off, Lincoln. I'm tired of this." She paced by him, pushing her hair up into a bun, and nearly screamed in frustration when she figured out she didn't have a hair tie. She slapped at her thighs and went back to pacing. "What exactly were you trying to achieve, Lincoln, bringing June to your house? Did you think I'd drop down on my knees and forgive the long absence with a blow job because you brought my childhood BFF back into my life? Well, think again, buddy. All you've done is put June's life in danger."

"I didn't bring her here, Roxie." He answered softly, trying to think of something to say to refute her belief that June was in danger now. The fact that she was his sister should keep her safe from anyone, no matter what Roxie's dad had been involved in.

"Yeah right. You just thought you'd push past the boundaries I insisted on in the contract, boundaries that are there for a good reason, and do as you pleased, because you're Lincoln Fucking Young. Again, fuck you, Lincoln." She didn't stop pacing but the glare she threw at him should have set his shirt on fire.

He wasn't going to say anything else, he'd decided, he'd just let her pace it out and wait until she calmed down, then he'd explain what had happened. Which was for the best considering she started right back up again.

"And I need to stop running? You have no idea what life has been like for me since that night. What about you, Lincoln? What are you running from? Because you're running from something. Your own truth, I expect, considering the way you've ignored me since we got back from Cambodia. You can't handle the fact that you care about me, so you ran. And that's probably why you brought June down here, knowing it'd just piss me off and I'd end things. Well, good for you, Lincoln. You've won."

She walked right up to him, her face coming up to his to make him look up from the floor he'd been staring at, clamping down on his anger the whole time. He looked into her eyes, eyes that had brought his heart back to life, and saw something he never thought he'd see - disgust.

"Piss off with your money, your trips, your every-thing, okay? Just fuck off and leave me the hell alone. I don't need your bullshit drama in my life, not when I have enough of my own to deal with. It was fun for a while, but whatever it is you think we've been doing? It's done now." She finished with a raised eyebrow, a quirk that asked if he dared to contradict what she'd said.

He didn't respond, she was too angry to listen to him right now. Instead, he left, closed her door, walked over to Tanya's car, and got in.

"What did you do, Mr. Young? I could hear her

shouting out here! Damn, you pissed her off good." Tanya said, letting him know the whole block had probably heard Roxie shouting at him.

"I didn't do anything, my sister did." He answered without thinking, shaken by the bitter anger Roxie had thrown at him, though he knew why she was angry.

It wasn't just June showing up, it was how he'd left her without much contact since they came back from a trip that had changed them both. That might have pissed her off even more than his sister taking his place at his house. But yeah, leaving June there without him had definitely not been a good idea.

"Keep an eye on her for me, I'm going home." He said what he'd meant to say when he first got in her car and left her there without another word.

He went back to his car, got in, and started to drive. How was he supposed to fix this? Did he want to fix it? Lincoln wasn't sure about either one but decided giving her some time to herself was the best idea.

June had said something about a conference so he knew the house should be empty now. He'd go back and let the ocean pound his body until his brain was numb. By the time the sun had set, and the moon came up, it was late, and June was back. She'd waved at him, tried to speak to him, but he barely mumbled two words at her. He was kind of pissed at her for just showing up like that.

It was only after she left, her head hanging down in defeat, that he admitted to himself that it wasn't really her fault that he had a secret he'd kept from her for a very long time. He'd hinted at it when she stopped eating and became so depressed, she'd lost weight she couldn't afford to lose, but he'd never answered another question about Chloe since then. She'd deserved to know the truth, but Chloe had disappeared on all of them, even him.

Besides, he'd been contemplating ending things with Roxie. That was why he'd agreed to go to New York with Kai, why he stayed in the city when he should have come back to Myrtle Beach. That was why he waited so long to ask to see her. His realization about how much he cared for her had shaken him and it was only now that he could really see that every step he'd taken had been to distance himself from her.

June had done that much better than he could have and he should probably thank her for that. If it didn't make him the world's biggest asshole, he probably would have. He couldn't hurt his sister like that though. He cared about her, in his own way.

He should probably go up, apologize to her, and explain things. She was sensitive, the most sensitive one of them all, she didn't deserve the way he'd treated her. She probably had a million questions about Roxie, but if Roxie had been as angry with June as she'd been with him, then she didn't get any answers at all. And she'd been giving a speech at that conference.

"I'm a shit brother and a shit whatever I was to Roxie. Fuck me." He mumbled and went back to the kitchen to get a beer out of the fridge. He'd spent long enough swimming to work off that hot dog, he'd do more tomorrow and get rid of any calories he'd consume from alcohol tonight.

It probably wasn't the best idea in the world to get drunk with Roxie at her old apartment, but he knew if he showed up at her place, or if she spotted him with Tanya outside her place, or spotted Tanya at all really, she'd blow a fuse. It was best to stay put and let Petey and Tanya do their jobs.

He found a remote and turned the music on outside. He didn't play it loud, he didn't want to bother his sister, but he did want to hear something besides his own breathing while he drank a beer on his deck. The sound of the surf mixed with the music to soothe him as he swung in a hammock that had been installed while he was in New York.

Life had become entirely shit lately and he didn't appreciate it a bit. He'd showered after his swim and changed into a white linen top with a pair of soft gray shorts, so he wasn't too hot, especially when a breeze kicked up.

This part wasn't so shit, he decided, but the rest of it?

Complete and total shit and with no clue how to fix any of it. He'd deluded himself when he thought he could walk back his relationship with Roxie to something a little more platonic. That wouldn't happen, not because of her, but because of him.

He couldn't look at her, even when she was angry and hurling hateful words at him, without thinking how beautiful she was. Yeah, he'd heard what she said, knew what she meant, but even then, his thoughts had been about how amazing she was. He'd wanted to calm her down and the only way he could think of to do that was to take away the focus of her anger - and that had been him.

Walking away wasn't weak, it was the only thing he could do. She might cool down, might forgive him at some point, might even let him explain things, but not when she was that much on fire.

He put a foot down on the deck, kicked a little to keep the swing of the hammock going, and replayed every moment he'd known her in his mind. From the moment he'd met her she'd been a star in his sky. Even when they were kids her smile had lit up a room unlike anybody else he'd ever known. And now? That smile could set hearts racing and blood pounding around the world, his included.

If only he could make it work. If only she wasn't so mad. But all the if onlys in the world wouldn't change their lives. Her parents had been murdered, as she'd long suspected, and those people were probably still after her. All he could do was try to protect her from those enemies, and the new enemies her ex-boyfriend had burdened her with. He'd do that, even if he had to do it from afar.

4

Roxie

"I'm so fucking done with him," Roxie growled to herself once Lincoln had stalked out of her apartment.

So what if the way he glared at her with those smoldering brown eyes nearly made her take all her words back? He was a complete asshole and seeing him after her little run-in with June just brought the fact home to her even more.

Frustrated and tired of what she had on, Roxie walked back to her bedroom to see if she had any clothes left that were worth wearing. She rummaged around in her drawers, noting that somebody, probably Wendy, had folded and put away whatever wasn't damaged. Once she changed into a pair of gray shorts and a black tank top, she felt much better. Twirling her hair up into a bun, she walked back out to her living room, inspecting everything as she went along.

Somebody had put a lot of effort into making repairs, she couldn't tell where the walls, floors, and everything else in the place had borne the brunt of her asshole ex's fury. Sure, the red velvet couch was new, but it was comfy and that made the loss of her old couch bearable. Going into the kitchen she was glad to see there weren't any new appliances, that was definitely Wendy's doing. They didn't really talk much about Roxie's aversion to electricity, but it was nice to know Wendy had respected her enough not to plug anything in or add to the list of appliances she wouldn't use.

The sound of a small fist knocking on the door brought Roxie's attention around to the entryway. She knew that knock and with a smile that was only a little strained, opened the door to see her friend.

"Hi, Wendy," Roxie said as she opened the door wider. Wendy had a bag full of food and drinks with her and that was all Roxie needed to know about what her friend might have heard earlier.

"I saw Lincoln leave and thought you might need a fixer." Wendy grinned and took the bag over to the new white coffee table in front of the couch. "I've got tacos, mozzarella cheese sticks, donuts, and cupcakes. Which do you want first?"

"The cake," Roxie said as she sat down on the couch beside her friend. "Did you get me water?"

"Of course." Wendy pulled items out of the bag and arranged them on the table. "I got some Dr. Pepper too, just in case."

"You know that's my totally-over-it drink. Damn, I love it." Roxie leaned into Wendy to nudge her a little and smiled ruefully. "What did I do to deserve you?"

"You moved above my parents' shop. And you're pretty awesome, too." Wendy's smile this time was a little shy but definitely pleased. She took a taco wrapped in paper and started to eat while Roxie had a turn at the chocolate cake nestled in a foam box.

They ate silently, Roxie not counting calories because she knew she'd work it off one way or another, just enjoying eating and being with each other. Roxie had a taco and a few cheese sticks before she sat back and opened the bottle of soda that she really did only drink on special occasions. Once she'd had her fill she sat back and looked over at her friend. "I guess you heard me yelling at Lincoln?"

"Not really, but the scowl on his face when he left told me all I needed to know." Wendy's lips pursed with grim amusement. "I knew you'd torn him a new one and probably with good reason."

"I did and I did." Roxie agreed and screwed the lid back onto the bottle. "I did not need the bullshit he put me through today. And no, I don't want to talk about it, but thank you for offering to listen."

Roxie knew the kind gesture of food and drink was Wendy's way of offering a shoulder to cry on. She loved Wendy, knew she could count on her to keep her secrets, but some secrets she didn't want to tell anyone. Her former life was something she'd hidden for a long time, revealing it now wasn't on her list of things to do.

"That's cool, just so long as you know I'll do whatever you need. I know there's people after you because of that asshole you used to date and if you need me to, I'll ship you off with a new passport with a fake name in one of the dry-cleaning trucks. There's a whole range of places you can go, if you want. Oh, and if you want to go to a foreign country, I can get you a passport and paperwork for one of those places too. I know a guy."

"I know you do," Roxie answered, remembering how terrified she was to use the last passport Wendy provided her. The little sucker had worked though, so she knew any others probably would too. She might need a different passport one day, a real one maybe, to get out of all of this mess. Maybe she'd go back to Cambodia, back to that little village where she'd been so at peace with the world. "You're a star, do you know that? And I'm not going to ask you what other secrets that innocent face of yours is hiding. I'm not sure I want to know."

Wendy just grinned a pearly white grin and winked at Roxie as an answer before she finished off the cheese sticks.

"So, are you coming back to stay here now?" Wendy asked nonchalantly but Roxie heard a hint of hope in her voice.

It was only then that she realized it had been a long time since she'd sat here with Wendy like this, when it used to be something they did once a week at least. And Lincoln had said she'd be safe here now, if she did. "Maybe. I'm not certain it's safe yet, but I'm definitely staying tonight. I miss my bed. And you."

"Aw, I knew you loved me." Wendy winked again and pulled her tablet out of another bag. "Movie?"

"Sure, I'm not in the mood to talk, but company sounds nice." Saying that wasn't hard, because she knew Wendy would understand. The other woman was kind, perceptive, and always a good friend. She'd do whatever Roxie needed.

Right now, that was distracting Roxie from her troubles with Lincoln. Somehow she doubted she'd heard the last of him, but she'd meant what she said. She was done playing games, being left in the dark, and living with total uncertainty. Maybe he was right to a degree, she decided as she watched Ryan Reynolds fight off ghosts gone bad with Jeff Bridges. She had been running for a long time and Nathan burning down Elmo's because he owed the wrong people money had given her even more reason to run.

Roxie's life since she was eighteen had been running from one bad situation after another. For a while, she'd thought Lincoln would make all of that different, would bring her some peace, but now? Now she thought that he only added to the stress she had to carry around with her. Roxie reached for a taco that was now cold, but still good, and munched on it. She wasn't really paying any attention to the film, but it didn't matter.

She'd managed to deal with far worse problems than the ones she was facing now, so she knew she'd find a way to get through this moment too. Eating her way through it wasn't the best choice, but if she was done with Lincoln, she'd have to go back to dancing, or teaching dance classes. Yeah, she had the money he'd paid her for teaching him about her world, but that wouldn't last forever. She'd have to get back out there tomorrow and hustle up some work. That was never really hard to do, but she'd rather not work in a dive bar. She was too good a dancer to go to one of those places.

Wendy was distracted by the movie and didn't notice Roxie sending a text, to find out if she could get back into giving dance classes. Kitty answered promptly, letting her know that the facility where Kitty taught classes would love to have her back. Roxie promised to call her friend the next day to set everything up and then tried not to touch her phone again. She half expected Lincoln to text her, to try to get her to listen, but her phone remained quiet.

Wendy left after the movie finished, claiming she had an early day and wanted to get some sleep, but Roxie had noticed the text Wendy got just before the movie ended and how wide Wendy grinned when she got it. Roxie let her friend have her secrets and thanked her for being so good to her with a hug.

Once the door was closed, the variety of locks and bolts set, and the lights out, Roxie sat back down on the couch and stared into the darkness. She might have been hasty in pushing Lincoln away, and hastier when she asked Kitty to find out if she could get a job with her, especially when Roxie had turned that down to give it to Kitty in the first place, but…had she really?

Lincoln wasn't ready for a relationship. He was still too independent and closed off for that. But then, so was she. She didn't want another boyfriend who would only use her and break her heart in the end. She'd had enough heartbreak over the years.

A thought tried to intrude, a smile on a face, but she put that thought away, back where it belonged, in the deepest part of her mind. More heartache she didn't want to remember tried to intrude as she sat there in the dark, trying to get a grasp on her feelings. It all served to remind her that relationships beyond friendship bring pain.

No, it would never work between Lincoln and her, she had to admit to herself as she went back to her bedroom and crawled beneath a sheet. It was hot in the room, but an open window brought in the scent of the ocean and hot tarmac. That smell had taken her a long time to get used to, but she had, and it smelled like home to her now.

Nathan had demanded she install an air conditioner in the room, or a fan at the very least, but she'd have missed that smell too much. Plus, they were prone to catching on fire if used incorrectly, or if they were faulty. It was better to be sweaty than crispy any day of the week.

Roxie pushed away the single sheet she'd pulled over herself and tried not to think about how much more comfortable Lincoln's bed was. Or how she could ignore her phobia and enjoy the central air that kept his house cool. Or how much she missed being beside him.

Her thoughts drifted to those hot nights in Cambodia and how he'd sneak into her tent at night. They'd always slept twined together, despite the heat, despite how sweaty they'd wake up. She'd become accustomed to having his body near hers and it was hard to fall asleep on her own, as she'd been doing since they got back.

It really sucked that he pulled that shit on her today. She had to think he'd done it on purpose. She had barely heard from him since they returned, but the one time he said he needed her, he'd sprung his sister on her instead of himself. Why would he do such a bullshit thing?

He told her she needed to stop running from the past, was that whole thing about forcing her to face it? He'd decided he knew what she needed better than she did and that really stung. Sure, he told her he wanted to learn to be a dom, but was invading her privacy part of what he thought a dom did? If so, then he thought wrong.

"Fuck, I can't sleep like this." She drawled into the empty darkness and got out of bed. Throwing her clothes off, she headed for the bathroom. Once the shower was cool, but not freezing, she stepped inside and let her thoughts disappear. Standing under the cool blast of water cleared her mind for a moment and her body relaxed.

She stood in there for a while but had to get out when the little bit of warm water she'd mixed with the cold disappeared. For a moment, she thought about going back to the hotel. She could tolerate the AC unit running in there, they had to be serviced regularly after all. But that meant driving in the middle of the night and she didn't have the energy.

Her phone would die if she tried to watch a movie, but she could probably get a couple of hours of reading out of it. She opened the app and tried to focus on the book she'd ordered. It was a suspense novel that soon had her in its grip, but sooner than she expected the battery warned her she was down to 15%. She'd have to take it out to her car in the morning and charge it.

She decided she'd go back to the hotel and get her stuff tomorrow too. Lincoln was a complete dick, but he was right about one thing: she had to stop running and get used to life in the apartment. She wouldn't be able to afford to keep both places if she was done with Lincoln and since he hadn't tried to contact her, she had to assume he was taking her seriously.

Not that she *wanted* him to plead his case to her. Not much, anyway. Okay, maybe a little bit. A text to feed her ego would have been nice, she thought with a grin that she quickly suppressed. She had to roll her eyes at her thoughts because she'd never been that childish or petty, but here she was, wishing Lincoln would be just a little bit miserable over losing her.

Instead, he respected her wishes. Which was good, she reminded herself, but at the same time, a little bit of pleading now that she was calm might have changed her mind. Or not. She never wanted to be wishy-washy, but shit with Lincoln was different.

Yeah, she was independent, able to take care of herself, and a fighter when she had to be. At the same time, Lincoln had turned her into a pile of mush that wanted to be acknowledged, that longed for his touch, that wanted to see him smile. Maybe he'd broken her. Was that it? Was she broken now?

5

Roxie

oxie woke up two days later to a couple of text messages from June. She hadn't heard from her friend the day after her exchange with Lincoln. That made Roxie wonder if Lincoln had talked with June about what happened. Maybe the woman who'd been her childhood best friend didn't want to talk to her now.

Maybe it had sunk in that Roxie was an exotic dancer and made her money in ways that a lot of mothers would never approve of, especially a woman like Lincoln and June's mother, Ms. Young.

Roxie got up and went into her closet to check for a change of clothes. She'd brought all her stuff over from the hotel, so her closet and drawers weren't as empty as they had been. She'd had to take some of her stuff down to the washer and dryer Wendy's parents kept in the back of the shop for her to use, but that was all done and put away now too.

After her shower, Roxie finally got up the courage to read the texts and picked up her phone to open them.

"Hey, I'm going back tomorrow. I decided to stay at a hotel and thought maybe you'd want to meet up before I go home. Want to meet me here?" June had asked in one of the texts. The next text was the name of the hotel and the address.

The hotel was one of the most exclusive in Myrtle Beach so it was a sure bet Roxie wouldn't run into anyone she knew. It wasn't one any of her friends owned so there was hope she'd remain anonymous at this place. With a happy smile on her face, Roxie texted June back and agreed to meet her at a café at the hotel.

She went back to her bedroom, put on a little makeup, found the Chanel dress she hadn't worn in what felt like months, and slipped into it. This one was a black viscose halter maxi dress with eyelet trim around the hem. Roxie turned in front of the mirror on her closet door, another new addition, and smiled at the effect the dress produced. She looked classy, sexy, and she liked that look. A pair of black Dior sandals finished off her ensemble and she was ready to go.

Roxie's drive was slow due to traffic, but she was

still in time for the meeting with June. She was nervous, even though she'd only just seen the woman a couple of days ago. June knew all her childhood secrets, about her crush on Liam, and all the other things she'd never admitted to anyone else. She also knew Roxie was originally born as Chloe. If she kept mixing up her name, June could make life difficult for her here, especially if they ran into someone Roxie knew.

Roxie reassured herself that she wouldn't meet anyone at the hotel who knew her from her life in Myrtle Beach, why should she? The James and Thompson families owned different hotels. They would never come to this place. Roxie shook out her dress once she'd turned the car over to a parking attendant, stood up straight in the flat sandals, and marched into the hotel with a fake smile on her face. This might just be a mistake, but she was going to fake her way through it if she had to.

Roxie quickly spotted the café and was on her way toward it when she spotted Kai. With June. Hmm. What was that about? The pair looked cozy, but they weren't touching. Roxie's grin turned into a slight smirk as she walked up to them.

"Hi, I'm here." She said loud enough for the pair to hear.

They pulled apart quickly and Kai looked up at

Roxie, confused. "I thought you said you were meeting that girl you used to hang out with, Chloe?"

Roxie's eyes turned sharply to Kai and then to June. She could have sworn he'd known who she was all along, but maybe not. And if he didn't, June had just inadvertently told him. She was a little annoyed about that, but June didn't know any better.

Roxie decided to save June the trouble of explaining and spoke up. "Roxie is my stage name, Kai. You don't remember me? Really?"

"No. I mean, I only met you once or twice back then, I think. I, uh..." He paused and gave them both a sheepishly chagrined look, "I wasn't at my most sober back then."

Which also meant that Lincoln hadn't clued him in to who she was either. Well, that was a point in Lincoln's favor at least, he'd kept her secret.

"It's okay." Roxie brushed off his unease and sat down. "I'm used to Roxie, so please use that, if you don't mind."

"Sure." June and Kai said in unison and Roxie hid another smirk as their cheeks turned a slight pink color. "So how are you both?"

"Fine." They answered in unison again. June brushed black hair behind her left ear and looked away from Kai.

"Have you been able to get ahold of Lincoln, Roxie? I haven't heard from him since the night I got here." June asked innocently but it still made Roxie's heart twinge a little.

Too many people knew her business, her past, her present, and it was all making her head whirl. Plus, Lincoln hadn't spoken to his sister or to Kai it would seem. That wasn't a good sign.

"No, we had a few words that same night and I haven't spoken to him since." Roxie picked up the menu to avoid looking at either of the people at the small table in the crowded café. It was a nice, open, light-filled space, but there were far too many people around, creating a buzz that should drown out anything she said, but meant there were more people that might notice her here.

"Oh. I've heard that Lincoln's real father wants to connect with him but every time I try to talk to Lincoln about it, he just shuts me down. It would be good for him to finally connect with the man. Then at least he could decide if he was better off not knowing him at all."

"Sorry, I have to go," Kai said after looking up from his phone. "Duty calls. It was lovely to see you both again."

June looked sad, but Roxie was a little relieved when the handsome man left. He was Lincoln's friend and might report back anything she might say to June. Men surely talked to each other, didn't they? Roxie kind of rolled her eyes at her own thoughts and the way June stared after Kai like a lost puppy that had been left without a home. Holy moly, June had it bad for Kai.

"Are you alright?" Roxie asked her friend when the seconds spanned into minutes and June didn't speak.

"What?" June looked as if someone had goosed her before she smiled and tried to brush it all off. "Yes, just lost in thought. What would you like to have?"

A waiter came to take their order and they waited until the two coffees were brought to them before they started to speak.

"Thanks for coming to see me. I've thought about you every second since I saw you at Lincoln's house. I've just been very busy with the conference, and well, now I'm leaving again but I wanted to see you, talk to you. I've almost wondered if that meeting was a dream." June smiled and reached out for Roxie's hand.

Roxie slid her right hand over to her friend, noticing how small her gold bracelet and the gold and emerald ring on her finger looked. Compared to the jewelry dripping off of June, Roxie's jewelry looked cheap. She'd never been one to flaunt her wealth, even when she had a rich daddy to buy her everything she wanted. Over the years she'd had very little money to buy more jewelry but the few pieces she owned were nice. But not as nice as June's.

"Stop comparing yourself to me," June said softly, for Roxie's ears only. "You're still more beautiful than I could ever be, no matter how much jewelry I might decorate myself in. You don't need it, believe me."

Roxie smiled ruefully, not surprised that June was still able to pick up on her thoughts. "I shouldn't do it, I just can't help it anymore, I guess. I've been broke for so long that I forgot what it was like to be anything else."

"I'd give you every piece I own if I thought it would make you happy, Roxie." June's eyes suddenly filled with tears that she quickly blinked away. "I've wondered what happened to you for so long, and now I know. I know we've gone over it, but I really am so pleased to have you in my life again."

"I am too," Roxie said automatically but smiled to let her friend know she meant it. "I've got a lot of things I have to deal with at the moment, but I promise, as soon as I'm free, we'll spend some time together. Or do you have a husband and family to get back to?"

"No, I never married, remember? And no kids, I've always been too busy for that." June dismissed it all with a wave of her hand.

"You're right, sorry." Roxie felt her own cheeks turn pink this time. "I don't know how I forgot that."

"You said it yourself, you've got a lot to deal with at the moment. And I hate to do this, but I'm about to add to it." June had the grace to look pained over what she'd said.

"What's up?" Roxie asked and leaned closer, concerned for her friend.

"Nothing major, really, I just..." Her words trailed off and she frowned. "I'm worried about Lincoln and you two seem to be friends at least, so I thought I'd talk to you about it. He's got a really weird view about relationships and part of that is Mom's fault, she never could seem to settle."

"Okay, what's any of that got to do with me?" Roxie assumed June was leading back to the whole Lincoln meeting up with his dad thing, but June surprised her.

"I just, well, Lincoln really should try to settle down, find a wife and have some babies. He wants a family in the future, he's even stored his sperm in one of our sperm banks along with some donor eggs he bought for future surrogacy. It's just, he's not happy." June emphasized the last word, making Roxie cringe.

"I'm not sure what you want me to do, June." She said, not wanting to look at her friend's face. She'd just ended things with Lincoln, and he hadn't said a word to her since. How was she supposed to explain that to his sister, and how was she supposed to help him?

"I don't know, I guess I just thought maybe you could talk to him about it all since he won't talk to me. All of that trauma with Mom marrying so many men didn't bother me as much, I saw how she loved my father, even if it didn't work out. He saw different sides to her than I did since he was born before me. And I saw your parents and how they loved each other, so I know what love is, but I don't think Lincoln does, and, well, I don't know. I'm just worried about him, that's all." June's words trailed off and she shrugged helplessly.

"He'll be okay, even if he doesn't marry, June. Not all of us want the happily ever after and the wedding bands with holy matrimony. I saw my parents, yours, I know love is real, but I can't convince someone that marriage is the life for them when I'm avoiding it myself." Roxie gave her own shrug and looked to her friend for understanding. "Does that make sense to you?"

"I guess so." June shrugged again, a frown chasing away the normal happy look to her features. "I don't understand why so many people are against traditional marriage nowadays, and it's my generation."

"Because there's so much more to life than procreation and giving money to banks when you buy a house, silly." Roxie teased her friend. June smiled and sighed deeply.

"I know, I'm not rushing to get married either, but I'd like my brother to be happy. Both of them, actually." June said, mentioning Liam by saying brothers.

Roxie let it go, the way she'd let her love for Liam disappear years ago, even if she'd kept that final love note from him. It was something from her past that she hadn't brought into the present, even if she still took that letter out sometimes, to remember old times and what it was like to be innocent.

"For what it's worth, I think Lincoln has exactly the life he wants to lead. Something tells me that if he was unhappy, he'd do whatever it'd take to fix that. If he's not fixing it, he's not unhappy." Roxie said, a little sharper than she meant to.

"You said you'd had words, does that mean you argued that day?" June took a sip of her coffee, frowned, and added another spoonful of sugar to the glass mug.

"Kind of." Roxie didn't want to admit why they argued, because of June herself, so she didn't want to talk about it too in-depth. "He made me really angry, and I let him know it. I'm not sure we'll be speaking to each other again, to be honest."

"Oh, I'm so sorry to hear that. You looked so happy before you realized it was me that day, I just assumed you two were together." June's face fell into sadness again and Roxie wanted to make it go away.

"You said yourself, Lincoln doesn't know how to love someone, or what love is, rather." Roxie corrected herself, wishing she hadn't added her own thoughts to June's words. "We were just friends, really."

"Friends that have had an argument. Well, I hope you two can make up with each other then. I'd like to see you both happy again. Even if it's not in *that* kind of way." June's smile brushed away the last remnants of sadness and Roxie couldn't help but smile with her.

"Well, your brother is a pig-headed jerk, so I wouldn't hold your breath, but you never know." Roxie felt like a traitor for giving June what she was certain was false hope, but she'd do just about anything to keep that smile on June's face. Just about anything. Maybe even talk to Lincoln again.

Roxie looked away from June, trying to hide the pain this conversation stabbed into her chest. June had confirmed what Roxie already knew, Lincoln might want a family, kids, but he didn't want a partner to love. He might just be incapable of it.

6

Roxie

"**O**kay, you have to pay attention to how I use my thigh muscles to control my descent," Roxie said, a month after her lunch date with June. "This will give you bruises so prepare yourselves."

She grinned as she relaxed the same muscles she'd just warned her students about and slid down the pole. A quick flex and she stopped with an almost painful grip on her skin. Yeah, there would be bruises.

Her captive audience clapped as if she hadn't just done something that wasn't second nature to her by now. They were new members of the dance studio so to them it probably did seem miraculous. She'd managed to get a few nights of teaching at the studio lined up and so far, quite a few students in. It was probably too soon to show them this move but they'd all begged Roxie to know how it was done so she'd agreed.

She let her thighs go and stopped herself just before she reached the floor. "We'll practice that move a little more later, but that should give you an idea of how it's done."

The ladies, all over eighteen and eager to learn, flooded around her to bombard her with questions. Roxie enjoyed their enthusiasm and was trying to answer them all when another face walked into the studio, one she was far too familiar with and hoped she'd never see again. Her stomach dropped and her throat went tight as someone grabbed her hand.

His face was almost black with anger, twisted with a rage she definitely didn't deserve. Roxie glanced back to see which of the ladies had her hand and saw it was a woman she knew as Keily. It didn't matter which of the women it was, it only mattered that one of them was there for her.

"You owe me, bitch!" Nathan shouted and the women that hadn't noticed him yet, all turned as one to face the savage voice.

"I don't owe you shit, Nathan. Get out." Roxie stood her ground in black stiletto boots, a pair of black denim shorts that barely covered her ass, and a loose white t-shirt. She felt powerful with those boots on, like she could stab his foot with one of the pointed heels. It helped that she had a wall of women behind her.

"I think you owe me quite a lot. I bought you shit while we were together." He paused, his eyes rolling up to the ceiling as if he were watching a bug fly around his head before he went back to speaking. "Yeah, I even bought you some tampons once. And other shit too. I want all of my money back."

He started to scratch at his neck like a dog with a bad case of fleas, which made the scowl and twisted look on his face seem totally harmless. Roxie knew she had to stand her ground, not just to show these ladies how to deal with unruly clients, but because backing down would make him bolder.

"Fuck off, Nathan. You got all the money you're getting out of me. I don't have any more to give to you. In fact, I have nothing else to give to you, so beat it. I've got a class to teach and you're in the way."

"I'm not leaving, Roxie. Not until you give me something." His face wasn't twisted anymore, it was filled with panic and a manic look in his eyes that made her wonder just how unbalanced he was. Or was it drugs? It was probably drugs.

Roxie gasped in surprise when he dropped to his knees and clasped his hands together. "Please Roxie. I just need enough for a fix. I mean, just something, anything. It hurts, Roxie, please?"

Roxie might have helped him if he'd admitted that he had a problem a long time ago, if he'd walked out of jail and into rehab, but this shit? No, she wasn't having it. "No, Nathan. Leave."

"You'd better leave, or I'm going to call 911 and get the law out here on your ass." Keily, a transplant from somewhere else in South Carolina if Roxie was remembering correctly, went full country on Nathan, right down to holding out her phone and waving it at him with her lips pursed and her blonde head tilted to the side.

"Nathan." Roxie started to say, but he didn't let her answer. Instead, he sprung up from the floor with a growl and slammed Roxie into the mirrored wall behind her. Roxie's head hit the glass so hard her ears rang, and the mirror shattered. She slid to the floor, her sight going dark around the edges until there was almost no light left at all.

"Look what you made me do, you bitch. You couldn't just give me some money, could you? You always thought you were better than me, even though you whore for a living." Nathan shouted, but Roxie didn't really hear him. Her head was spinning.

"Hello, I'd like to report an assault." Roxie heard Keily say, but then the other women were shouting and screaming, and from the sounds she heard, Roxie was certain that a few kicks and punches landed somewhere on Nathan. Her students were dragging him out of the studio, their banshee screams of anger filling the building.

Keily finished on the phone and then rushed to sit down by Roxie. Gentle fingers probed at her head and then tugged at her chin. "You okay, honey?"

"I feel sick to my stomach." Roxie drawled thickly, her head splitting now.

"I think you've got a concussion. The ambulance will be here soon."

"I can't go to the hospital, no insurance," Roxie murmured and tried to get control of her senses. "I'm fine, I just need some ice and to sit here for a minute."

"I understand. It's tough when you don't have insurance." Keily looked at her with understanding, her pretty eyes sad for Roxie. "Let me see what the other women are doing and find a first aid kit."

"It's on the wall in the office, behind that closed door." There was only one, Roxie remembered, and hoped there was an ice pack in the thing. She'd never opened it and didn't know.

Keily came back just as a local police patrol car arrived outside. An ambulance followed a few minutes later after Roxie told the story of what had happened for the first time. Of course, it was asshole Detective Slater's bitchy ass that showed up, but at least this time she didn't sneer at Roxie like she was wasting her time.

"I'm glad you called to report this, it's been a while since we had any news on him. I'd started to think he left the state." Detective Slater said as she wrote something down and walked away to let the ambulance driver have a look at Roxie.

Roxie let the female paramedic check her over but refused to go to the hospital. The paramedic tried to urge her to go, which forced Roxie to be blunt. "Look, I can't afford the ride in your shiny little medical taxi out there and I certainly can't afford the hospital bill. If I get worse, I'll have someone drive me to urgent care or something."

Not that urgent care was really any cheaper, but she didn't have a whole lot of choices.

"Sure, yeah, I understand." The woman looked a little miffed, but she smiled at Roxie. "I hate that some people fall through the insurance cracks, but I understand. Take care of yourself."

"Thanks. Have a good night." Roxie said automatically, her eyes closed as the ice pack Keily brought to her earlier worked to ease some of the pain in her head. "I think I just need a dark room and more ice."

"Don't fall asleep. Have someone stay with you tonight, just in case, alright?" The paramedic replied and walked off.

"Let me take you back to my place, my husband and I just moved out here with our babies. I'd like to keep an eye on you for a few hours and I'd love some company." Keily reappeared now that she'd given her own account of the incident. The other ladies were outside with the police, giving their own statements. "I asked if I can take you home and that bitchy cop said I could."

Roxie smiled through the pain at the chirpy woman with a big smile. Her gray eyes begged Roxie to agree and for once in her life, Roxie agreed to let someone else take control for a minute of her life. She just couldn't say no to that look. "Alright. But only for a little while."

"Great, let me help you up," Keily said.

Once they'd both gathered their bags and Roxie ensured Kitty was going to close up the studio for the evening, Keily guided her out to a very expensive and luxurious SUV. Roxie tried not to gape at the control panel in the middle of the console, but Keily must have caught her.

"It's my husband's idea of a present. We have triplets and he's really protective of all of us. He hunted down the safest vehicle he could for us." Keily smiled over at her and then put the big SUV in gear.

Roxie didn't even know what the make of the thing was but had a feeling it was foreign and far more expensive than she thought it was. It didn't really matter right now, anyway. It was just nice to let someone else drive and worry about evening traffic. Moments from the incident kept replaying in her head though, the way

Kitty and her whole class had rushed into Roxie's side of the studio, the way all of the women piled on Nathan to throw him out. He'd managed to escape them and run off and Roxie could only hope that was the last time she'd see him.

Roxie opened her eyes when she felt the vehicle stop and noticed the engine was off. Her eyes found a huge white stucco mansion not that far from Lincoln's place. She'd passed it several times as she drove back and forth from his home. That set her nerves on edge, but she doubted she'd see Lincoln at this time of day. He was probably still at work or home, cooking something to eat for himself.

"Nice place," Roxie said as she opened the door and got out, her bag over her shoulder.

"Thanks, we like it. We decided we wanted to be closer to the ocean, Logan loves it and I thought it might be a nice place for our girls to grow up." Keily unlocked the front door with a code entered on a keypad and showed Roxie in.

"I'm back," Keily called out as she led Roxie deeper into the house. A foyer with marble floors drifted into a recessed living room with a view of the sea. "Have a seat, I'll get us some water."

"Thanks," Roxie murmured and went to sit down on a dark blue leather sectional.

Keily wandered off in the direction of the kitchen,

Roxie assumed, and came back with two bottles of water and two glasses filled with ice. "That seat you're on reclines. Put your feet up and relax for a little while."

"Thanks," Roxie said and felt her cheeks turn red. She was repeating herself now.

"I'm sorry that happened to you," Keily said softly, not looking at Roxie as she spoke. She filled the water glasses instead and handed one to Roxie. "Will you be okay if you go home? I have lots of extra bedrooms if you need one."

"No, that's too much to ask." Roxie refused immediately but softened it with a smile. "I should be fine if I go home. I haven't lived with Nathan in a long time. I'm sorry you all had to see that."

Roxie made a mental note to send all of her students an apology and one to the owner of the studio. None of them deserved to see that.

"Well, it's not your fault some psycho asshole intruded on our class. Some people just don't know how to take no for an answer." Keily frowned and got up to walk over to a closet. She opened it, took something out, and came back to sit down. "This is a taser designed by my husband and his company. Keep it with you."

"Oh, cool, thanks." Roxie looked at the small device and saw it was small, but no doubt packed a punch. It would fit into her back pocket nicely.

"I have plenty of them so if you want more just ask."

Keily looked over at Roxie and frowned. "Are you sure you'll be alright if you go home?"

"Oh yes, I'll be fine." Roxie nodded her head and remembered why she was there. Her skull had nearly cracked earlier because of Nathan.

"Alright. Well, my girls are asleep and dinner's ready. Do you feel like eating? Logan's in California on business tonight so it'd be nice to have some company, if you want?" Keily's almost fairy-like beauty and the appealing nature of her smile made it an offer Roxie couldn't refuse.

"The stomach wobbles are gone, and the headache is down to a dull throb. I might be able to manage a meal." Roxie got up and followed Keily into a dining room with an outer wall made of windows and an inner wall painted white. A long table was set for two and food was already on the table.

"This is a really nice place," Roxie said, staring out at the ocean. It must be nice to live here.

"It's more than I deserve, let me tell you. I got lucky with my husband." Keily sat down across from Roxie at the end nearest the door and reached her hand out to a bowl of salad and a roasted chicken with vegetables in small bowls around it. Every dish was white, clean, and bright.

"What do you mean?" Roxie asked, curious as to how much Keily would talk.

"He's my second husband and we knew each other in high school. I was this awful cheerleading beauty queen and he was the poor kid that couldn't catch a break. He showed us all though, by becoming a really successful businessman. I married the quarterback of our high school but came to regret that. I got divorced and Logan came along. We reconnected and here we are."

"That sounds like a good story," Roxie replied, adding chicken to her plate and some of the salad.

"Oh my, it is, and I love him dearly. Which is partly why I joined your class. I want to impress him in the bedroom and out of it." Keily winked at her, a dirty but fun-filled grin.

"I like this story already, go on." Roxie started to eat and was soon drawn into the story.

7

Roxie

"I was a terrible kid, an even worse wife, and I had a lot to make up for, but Logan is a good man, and my sister is really incredible. She'll be coming out in a couple of weeks to visit me." Keily changed the subject for a second, before she picked the thread back up. "It's the Logan part that I want to really work on. He loves adventures, and I'm always eager to please him, especially if it pleases me at the same time."

Roxie smiled, understanding that Keily was a kindred spirit almost instantly. One day Keily might actually go into detail about the previous part of her story, but Roxie wouldn't push. People told their stories best when they were allowed to do it in their own time.

"So, what about you? Have you always lived out

here?" Keily asked her, making Roxie tense, but she knew it was only curiosity.

"No, I'm a transplant, like so many others. A refugee from the cold winters in the north. I grew up living in places like New York. There's a lot of snow there." Roxie was taken aback by how Keily's eyes went wide with surprise. People always reacted like that, but it still confused Roxie, every time.

"You left New York to come *here*?" Keily looked even more confused, but Roxie understood. Most people thought that Myrtle Beach was some Podunk beach resort town for hooligans, but it was so much more than that. It was a place where dreams came true for many, a shining beacon on the coast that lit up the dreams of kids in the mountains, far from the ocean, and so many other places.

"Of course! Why wouldn't I? New York was cold, dirty, full of hateful people. Here I have the beach, the sun, and all the salty air I can stand. And it's so much warmer in the winter than it is up there." Roxie laughed at herself a little as Keily shook her head.

"I understand. You have the southern accent down so you must have lived here for a while." Keily's face maintained the curiosity and open friendliness.

"A while, yeah." Roxie hedged, trying to think of an answer other than 'that's part of my disguise'. "It's infectious, that slow, drawling accent."

"I guess." Keily's answer wasn't judgmental, just doubtful. "I've grown up hearing it every day of my life but apparently people like how we talk in the south."

"It's much nicer than what I grew up hearing, believe me," Roxie assured her. Even with a private school education and rich friends, the northern accent she'd grown up hearing was harsh and grating compared to the slow and easy accent she'd fallen in love with instantly.

"So why are you teaching pole dancing classes and not working?" Keily asked, changing the subject to something Roxie was much more comfortable with.

"Well, I used to work at the best club you could find in town, but that was before it burned down. I can take you to the second-best club one day, if you'd like?"

"Wait, the best one burned down? What happened?" Keily leaned forward, eager to be filled in.

"You know that guy at the studio today? He's the reason it burned down. While I was working there, actually."

"Whoa. You've got to tell me all about it." Keily was nearly bursting with excitement and Roxie smiled at the eager display.

"Well, it turns out he had a gambling problem and decided that I'd get a lot of money out of an insurance policy if he set it on fire. The problem was, it was obvious it was arson and because of that, the insurance company is balking at paying out the policy. Roxie explained what had happened, surprised at how wrapped up in the story Keily became. "I was planning on starting a new club somewhere else, when the insurance company started dragging their feet, putting the kibosh on my plans."

"Wait, are we just talking about an exotic dancing club, or something more? I'm not judging, I just want to be sure I understand you." Keily asked, her gray eyes alight with delight.

"Well, it would be a mixture of things. We'd have the dancers, of course, but there'd be rooms for people to use to fulfill their fantasies, either together or with other members of the club. If they wanted to make arrangements with one of our dancers there'd have to be a contract and the dancer has to give their approval. That part is very important."

"Ah, I see." Keily didn't look as if she'd changed her mind about wanting to know more about what she had in mind, so Roxie went on.

"I'd like to hold competitions with dancers from all over the world coming to take part in the contests. That would be something new that we didn't do at Elmo's. I want to expand on what we had there and move into other areas of that world." Roxie revealed, wondering if she was talking too much but unable to stop.

"That sounds like it would be fun!" Keily said, still

full of eager delight. "And there'd be private rooms that people could rent out, you said?"

"Yes, so we'd need staff to keep those clean. Everything has to be sterilized, so staff would have to be trained to do that. But the rooms would be for members and employees only. Men or women, anybody. I don't want this place to be for the male gaze only, I want everybody to get what they want out of the place. I'd even like to find some male dancers."

"Oh, you mean like Magic Mike style dancers? Yes please!" Keily nodded her head vigorously. "I love watching women dance, but men can be just as hot."

"Yeah, just like Magic Mike, but I doubt I'd ever get Channing Tatum to dance there. It would be nice, though." Roxie winked at Keily who laughed with pure delight.

"I don't know, but I'd pay good money to see him dance live," Keily said, her eyebrows wiggling over her eyes.

"I would too."

"Hmm. I have an idea." Keily had a huge grin on her face as she looked at Roxie.

"What's that?" Roxie asked, suspecting a plan for the club might be on the way. She wasn't sure that was what was happening and warned herself not to get too excited yet. Keily might just be about to tell her about some club she knew about, for all Roxie knew.

"Well, I'd be really interested in something like that. Not just investing, but maybe even helping to run it. I'll have to discuss it with my husband, but I think we might be able to work something out." Keily said, offering hope to Roxie of getting her life back on track as if she'd offered her the loan of a car to go to the grocery store and not something truly life-changing.

"Really?" Roxie asked, wondering if she had been knocked out and this magical woman was all part of some dream. This couldn't be real, could it? People like this didn't just randomly show up in real life. Well, not in Roxie's experience anyway.

"Yeah, I'm not joking. I'd really like to do something like this with you." Keily shook her head and leaned back, thinking about possibilities if the gleam of excitement in her eyes meant anything.

"I can't believe you're real or that we've only just met properly. I have some sketches back home, ideas I've had for decorating the place. I'll have to bring them to you at some point and see what you think." Roxie didn't want to get ahead of herself, but she was eager to get this off the ground, even if her head had started to thump again. She gingerly brushed her fingers over the lump and tried to make it stop hurting, but the numbing effect of the ice pack was already wearing off.

"I'm glad you've got some ideas. I don't know where

to even start. What about safety and health stuff? Will that be difficult here?"

"Well, I'd like a more exclusive club to start with. Even more exclusive than Elmo's was. And yes, they take health and safety very seriously here, as they should in places like that. People might have to pay more to become a member than they did at Elmo's, but the extra fee will be worth it. I want my girls to be healthy and safe and we'd have to maintain the same requirements for our clients. That's one of our top priorities, I don't want sick employees because we're lax, and I definitely don't want people like Nathan being able to walk in and set the place on fire all over again. I want identity checks on the clients that join the club."

"I get that." Keily nodded, her gaze turned inward, thinking. "I think we'll have to have a meeting, discuss the financials and figure out where to even put the club, but yeah, I think we could work something out."

"Awesome. I really can't believe this."

The conversation gave Roxie some hope, but she wouldn't hold her breath. People couldn't always come through for you, no matter how much they wanted to. Keily seemed really interested in having a clean, safe place for Roxie and her girls to dance in, but again, Roxie wasn't going to hold her breath.

"Well, I'm not promising anything right now, but I think Logan will be interested in this too. And my babies are at an age where I can put my degree in business to good use without it being too painful for us all." Keily's smile wasn't just full of pride because of her babies but in herself too.

"Good for you, getting a degree," Roxie said, impressed with the other woman. She was on her second marriage, but she'd earned a degree and given birth to triplets. That was impressive.

"Oh, it's not that big of a deal, but I'm proud of it. So, who are the dancers you have in mind? Do any of them work at the studio? That Kitty woman, for instance?" Keily asked, moving the conversation on.

Roxie smiled and noted how good Keily was at steering the conversation away from herself. She let it pass, though.

"Yeah, Kitty would be one of the girls I'd want. I'm still in touch with most of the dancers. Most of them are afraid of going back to work in the other clubs, because even with our security at Elmo's, Nathan still managed to fool them all to get in and that makes them nervous. Someone that we all trusted almost killed us and burned down our workplace. It's hard to trust anyone after something like that."

"I bet." Keily nodded, her eyes full of sympathy. "It must make it hard in all aspects of your life, especially since you were with him."

"It's not been easy." Roxie sighed, the pain in her

head increasing. Nausea started to intrude, and she closed her eyes.

"How about I drive you back to your car? You look completely done in." Keily suggested kindly and Roxie smiled.

"Yeah, I think I need to get home and take care of this head of mine," Roxie answered, opening her eyes.

"Well, let's get you back then." Keily got up and held her hand out to Roxie.

Roxie took the woman's hand and looked at her with wonder. "You're incredible."

"I can tell you for nothing that you wouldn't have said that if you'd met me when I was with my first husband, but I'm trying." Keily shrugged and led Roxie out of the house.

Roxie managed to drive herself home once Keily dropped her off and knew that Wendy would be up soon. Roxie was later than normal getting home but she'd enjoyed talking with Keily so much that she'd barely been able to pull herself away. She let herself in, put the bottle of water and ibuprofen she'd got on the way home on the coffee table, and slumped onto her couch.

She was too tired to even take off the stiletto boots as she picked up a sketchbook from the coffee table and flipped it open. It was filled with design ideas she'd had for a new club, something far more exclusive than

Elmo's, with much better security. She'd told Keily Elmo's had been the best, but there was always room for improvement.

With a faint smile, she picked up her phone and started to reply to Wendy's last text. She'd explained in texts to Wendy before she came home that Nathan had caused a problem at work but hadn't explained fully.

The last text from Wendy nearly made her have a heart attack.

"I heard you were injured? You better call me right now!" That wasn't what made Roxie's blood pressure go up, though. It was that the text came in more than a half-hour ago. Wendy would be panicking. Roxie cursed herself for not calling and explaining. She was typing a text when a knock came at the door.

8

Roxie

"What the fuck are you doing here?" Roxie glared at the person blocking her front door, her face schooled into a frown. Roxie's eyes moved when she saw a face pop up at the bottom of the stairs before it flashed away. Wendy.

Wendy had called him when she didn't respond. But then again, her friend must have called him before she got home if he was only just getting here. She'd deal with that little traitor later. For now, she had one very concerned-looking man on her doorstep to deal with.

"I heard about Nathan showing up at the studio. Are you alright?" Lincoln had been frozen in place when she opened the door, his eyes scanning her for injuries. Now he barged in, brushing past her with his head swiveling, looking around for threats or something.

"He's not here, Lincoln. I'm fine. Now get the fuck out of my apartment." But a sudden burst of pain in her head and waves of nausea made her skin go pale as she winced.

"You are not alright. Sit down." Lincoln glared at her until she did just that. Once she was off her feet, he pulled out his phone to text someone.

She probably didn't want to know what the message was or to whom he'd sent it, so she didn't bother to ask. Glaring at him didn't cause a reaction and neither did sighing deeply as she crossed her arms and legs. He wasn't getting the hint at all.

"I don't want you here, Lincoln. Please leave." She tilted her head with care not to aggravate the lump on her head and motioned at the door with her eyes. "Go."

"No. Listen. I'm stupid, I know that and I'm sorry." He sighed, plowing his hands through his hair as he sat down on the floor in his expensive suit. "I can't lose you, Roxie. Not now that I know who you are, who you really are under all the facade. I've tried to leave you alone, tried to think of ways to make what happened with my sister up to you, but I've come up blank. I have no idea what to do to make all of this better. Please? Don't make me leave."

The reminder of why she'd broken things off with

him didn't do him any favors, she thought as her lips pursed a little harder. "Really?"

"What?" He asked blankly, his soulful eyes on hers. He looked so worried, hurt, sad, and all the other emotions she'd avoided for so long as he waited for her answer that she almost caved.

Could he be capable of more than she and June gave him credit for? She stared at him on her floor and had to wonder if what he'd said was true. Did he really care for her? Miss her? She wanted to believe him, but there was a small voice in the back of her mind telling her to run if he wouldn't get out of her home.

"You think just showing up and throwing an apology at me is going to make me change my mind?" She glared with eyes narrowed to slits, but he didn't burst into flames. Unfortunately.

"I don't know what will make it better, Rox, because I have a feeling this goes a lot deeper than *you can't trust me*." He shut up quickly when she leaned forward, her eyes two blue shards of ice. "I want you to move in with me."

"No." She sat back, arms and legs crossed defensively again, and refused to budge. She'd kill Wendy with a death-glare later for this. Her friend meant well, yeah, but this was too far. It was bad enough dealing with Nathan today, now she had to deal with Lincoln too? "It's better we end this now, before either one of us gets hurt any worse than we already are."

"No." He answered and got up. He went into her bedroom and started making noise in there. She got off the couch in a rush but had to stop when her stomach let her know that was a bad idea. Once the urge to throw up had passed, she made a move for her bedroom.

"What the fuck do you think you're doing?" She asked as she walked with careful steps into her bedroom to find him packing her suitcases. "Put that shit back, right now, Lincoln!"

"No." He replied and took the loaded cases to the front door. Somebody knocked at the door and Lincoln opened it. Wendy was there, doing her best to blend into the background. That must have been the text he'd sent. He'd made the decision for her before he'd even spoken to her properly, the bastard.

"Traitor!" Roxie growled at her cowering friend. She could feel the way her cheeks glowed red but that wasn't from embarrassment. She was well and truly pissed off now. "Lincoln, stop this right now. Put my clothes back."

"No." He handed the cases over to Wendy and came back to stand in front of Roxie. His face was a stony mask as he looked down at her. "Brace yourself."

"For what?" But the words oofed out of her as he picked her up and put her over his shoulder.

"Fuck! Lincoln, put me down. I'm going to be sick!"

Roxie cried but he just slapped her bottom gently. "Lincoln, I'm warning you."

But he didn't put her down. He just kept walking and he was almost to the door but went back to pick up her phone as she pummeled his back and protested.

"Put me down, you asshole. This is kidnapping."

"No, it's not. You want to go. You just won't admit it because you're stubborn as hell. Now, be quiet and get in the car." Lincoln's voice buzzed from his chest into her lower abdomen in a most delightful way, but Roxie wouldn't admit it to him. Her head swam as he walked down the stairs to his car.

"Fuck you, Lincoln Young. I fucking hate you. Now, put me down." Roxie said as he bent to lower her into the car. She noted it was the backseat and his driver was in the front, ready to sweep them away. Convenient. He'd probably had that planned out too, the asshole.

"Move over. I hate you too, by the way. Now, move over. Let me in." Lincoln's body was half in the car and half out. He looked at her as if he really expected her to be complicit in her own kidnapping.

Roxie glared at him and thought really hard about kicking him. She still had the stiletto boots on though. She'd hurt him badly if she kicked him with those. Was that a bad thing, she considered for a moment before she moved over.

"I'm a grown woman, Lincoln. You can't tell me what

to do." She crossed her arms over her chest and glared out the window. What she didn't do was open the door and get out the other side. She told herself it was because that door was probably locked, but she didn't even try it to see if it was.

"This is so not cool, Lincoln." She mumbled without looking at him. "You didn't even get my toothbrush."

"I have extras at the house." He brushed off her protest, and she could feel his eyes on her, checking to see if she was alright.

"Fine. And stop staring at me." She knew she should protest harder, she should do whatever it took to get out of this car, but she couldn't make herself.

She'd missed him so much it hurt, even if she'd had to hide that pain even from herself. She'd kept busy, doing private gigs when she could, but every night the pain had crept in. The loneliness of sleeping without him, only him, had plagued her. She'd taken to drinking a few shots of vodka before she crawled into bed, but even the alcohol hadn't taken away the misery of not sleeping beside him.

This was probably another mistake, she'd probably end up back at her apartment even more broken than she was now, but she couldn't make the words leave her lips that would end this stunt of his. She couldn't say brutal, cruel things to him, lies that would make him take her back home and never come back. She just couldn't do it. So she glared out of the window, angry more with herself than him.

When they got to his house Roxie pushed open the door of the car and walked into the house. It wasn't any different from the last time she was there, except his sister wasn't there this time. She walked into the kitchen, grabbed a glass from the cabinet, and filled it with ice and water. When he came into the kitchen, she glared at him again.

"How do you propose we make this work, Lincoln?" She looked up when he walked over to her, ready to browbeat him into taking her home if he couldn't convince her. Instead of speaking though, he kept walking until he had her in his arms, wrapped in the safest place she'd ever been.

"This is how, Roxie. This is how we make this work." He kissed the top of her head when she didn't go stiff or push him away.

She was enjoying being in his arms again too much to protest. But she couldn't stay quiet. "Sex won't cure everything, Lincoln."

"I'm not talking about sex, Roxie. I'm talking about being here for each other, about honest emotions, not the ones we show everybody to hide what's really going on inside. When I asked you to introduce me to your world, you weren't completely honest, were you? You said I had to be willing to push boundaries, that I had to be open to what you introduced to me. But you never said this could happen."

"I did warn you that emotions could get in the way if you weren't careful." She protested, tears in her eyes for some stupid reason. She tried to blink them away but that only made them fall harder. "I told you I don't do emotions."

"Ah, but that was a lie, my dear. It seems we both do." He held her tighter, but then let her go. "Will you stay?"

It was a simple question but there was so much more behind it. She took a deep breath, swiped at her eyes, and looked at him. He was right, whether she wanted him to be or not. She...*felt* something for him and it seemed he did for her too. Even if she'd walked away from that lunch date with June believing he was incapable of loving someone. "I still hate you."

"And I hate you, too, Roxie. I hate you so much it seems I can't sleep without you." He smiled, an expression that should convey happiness, but it barely reached his eyes. "Please?"

"Fine." She took a sip of her forgotten water and refused to look at him. This conversation was harder than she could have ever imagined it would be. Looking at him only made it harder. "But we have to fix this."

She waved a finger between her body and his to emphasize her point. "Whatever this is, we have to fix it. No more surprises, first of all."

"Not like that, no." He agreed with a nod of his head. "I didn't do that setup with June on purpose, by the way, she just showed up. Something my family is in the habit of doing when they find out I've bought a new place they want to use. I panicked when I saw her and left. I should have warned you."

"I see." Something about the way he said it made her believe him. "Cool. I understand."

"Good." He walked over to her and stood in front of her but didn't hug her again. That was a little disappointing. "How is your head?"

He'd talked to more people than just Wendy then. Roxie wondered if he'd talked to Kitty or somebody else from the studio to get that information because she hadn't told Wendy about the lump on her head.

"It's sore, really sore, and my stomach is rebelling again." She answered, her hand over her stomach as if that would calm it down.

"I'll make you some toast. Or do you want something else?" He looked at her and waited.

A faint smile tugged at the corners of her lips, and she felt a warm sensation on her cheeks. She had no clue why she was blushing just because Lincoln offered to make her toast, but she was.

"No, toast sounds good." She shrugged, not really feeling hungry but food might help. It was also a distraction from her pink cheeks.

Lincoln went about making the toast while Roxie went to the table and picked her phone up from where he'd put it down. She sent one text. It went to Wendy.

I'm going to kill you tomorrow.

Wendy sent back a slew of emojis that ranged from an angel to a crying laughing face and a text message. *Sorry, but you know you love me. You'll thank me one day.*

Doubtful, Roxie thought with a mental growl, but as Lincoln put a plate of toast in front of her and sat down, she had to admit she felt better already. Safer. Happier even.

"How is it?" Lincoln asked when she finished her first piece of toast. He'd watched her like he'd prepared a gourmet meal and needed her approval.

"My stomach or the toast?" She asked after a sip of water, not giving anything away.

"Both? Your head? All three?" He smiled at the way he fumbled for an answer, and she grinned despite herself.

"It's all fine. I had some aspirin for the headache and that's kicking in." The toast was dry, but she wouldn't complain. Butter or margarine might be too oily for her stomach right now. "Can I have a shower?"

"Of course. Go ahead, you know where everything is, I'll take your bags upstairs."

She wanted to protest again, demand he take her home. The words 'you can't do this' were on the tip of her tongue, but she couldn't make her throat work to actually speak. Which could only mean one thing.

She was where she'd wanted to be all these weeks and now that she was here, she didn't want to leave. "I'm not quitting my job. I've only just got it back."

"That's fine, Roxie. Do as you please. But I will be posting someone to watch over you while you're there from now on." He said it in a way that left no room for argument. He stared at her, unblinking, until she nodded her head in agreement. "Good."

Roxie walked up to the bathroom she always used when she was at Lincoln's place and got in the shower. Luckily, the skin hadn't broken when the mirror shattered under her head so there were no cuts to deal with as she washed her hair. Just a lump to remind her how different Lincoln was from Nathan.

She walked out of the bathroom and wheeled her suitcases to an empty bedroom. She might have given up on convincing him to take her home tonight, she might have enjoyed that hug, but she wasn't sleeping in his room or with him. She stared out of the dark window, not happy with herself, but also fighting a little glow of happiness that she was back in Lincoln's home. He wasn't far away, and that sense of security she felt when she was with him was back.

Despite her better judgment, she was staying and that…made her smile.

9

Lincoln

Lincoln was still at work when his PA, Tanya, called to tell him there'd been an incident at the studio where Roxie worked. Then she dropped a bomb and told him that Nathan was involved. Lincoln knew it was all being taken care of, Tanya let him know the paramedics and police went to the scene, so he stayed put. Roxie didn't want him in her life right now, he'd stay cool.

Then Wendy had texted to tell him she couldn't get through to Roxie. Hoping she'd be at the apartment by the time he got there, he left work and raced to the only place he could think of that she might be at. His brain had been running on fumes since the day his sister showed up at his house, but it geared up into overdrive on the way to her apartment.

He didn't want to lose her again. He'd lost her once, ten years ago, and when he found her again, he didn't want to let her go. It was in Cambodia that he discovered just how much he needed her in his life. Anything could have happened there, especially when that storm came through, but they'd weathered it together and no trees had fallen on her to take her from him. But then his sister intruded and that really did change everything.

Roxie had been furious with him, and although he hadn't done anything on purpose, he had left his sister there without telling Roxie. She was right to be angry with him since he'd just run off and avoided explaining anything to either of the two women, really. June was probably pissed at him too since he hadn't told her he knew where Chloe/Roxie was. That must have taken a lot of explaining, if Roxie explained anything at all to his sister.

He still didn't know what had happened there.

Roxie was in the shower now and all he could think about was getting in there with her, but he doubted she'd appreciate that. She was still furious and after her run-in with Nathan, anything that hinted at sex would probably have her running away again. Not that she was afraid of sex, but yeah, he didn't think she'd go for it.

He didn't say a word when she went to the bedroom

she'd used when she first stayed with him. For now, he was just happy knowing where she was. Over the next few days, he moved most of his work from the office to the house. Even his PAs worked at the house now. They were virtually camping in his kitchen, and both doted on Roxie.

He even conducted most of his meetings over Zoom, just so he could stay home with Roxie. Instead of going out to eat, he ordered food from the best restaurants and Kai ended up being so concerned over Roxie, and Lincoln's behavior over what had happened, that he sent down some of his mother's magical healing soup. It was some kind of chicken soup with herbs and mushrooms. Roxie liked it, even if she wasn't really sick.

Lincoln didn't know how to explain this sudden concern over her health, her condition as he kept calling it, even though everyone responded to that by asking if Roxie was pregnant. No, he'd try to explain, it was more to do with how she'd responded to the assault. It bothered him that she didn't seem to be put out at all. As if this kind of thing happened so often it didn't phase her.

That wasn't normal and it had him worried. He ordered the best food he could to help her be strong and healthy, but he wasn't sure what to do about her reaction to all that shit with Nathan. The fact that she seemed unphased really, really got to him. Had her life been that bad that an assault by a former boyfriend went by without even a blink of upset?

Now he was about to take some sushi from Kai's New York restaurant to her. Going to the actual restaurant would cost him at least $800 a person, having it shipped down on a private jet had cost him even more. It was all worth it though, to see her smile.

Lincoln got out of the car his driver parked in his driveway and headed into the house. It was good to have his driver back, even if he wasn't doing much back and forth between house and office right now. His driver hadn't been living in South Carolina so having the time to work hadn't really been possible before he'd moved his office to his house. Now his driver had relocated and Lincoln welcomed him back into the work-family with relief.

What made him even happier in life was currently sitting on his couch, looking bored as she scrolled through Netflix looking for something to watch.

"Binged your way through Lucifer, have you?" Lincoln asked, heading into the kitchen with a huge white catering box.

"I'm saving the last season for hard times." She said, her voice as bored as her face. "Although, this might qualify as hard times."

Lincoln grinned as he unboxed eel sushi along with a few other selections, put some of the condiments Kai sent in the box into a bowl, and grabbed some chopsticks from a drawer. "Well, if you're bored with life that much, let me bring you something that will brighten your day."

He set the plate down on the coffee table in front of her and sat back to watch her face.

"You went for sushi? I thought you were going to the airport for something?" She sat forward, inspecting the plate and the wasabi and sliced ginger in bowls.

"I did - this." He held his hand out to indicate the plate and smiled at her confusion.

"You got me airport sushi? Are you sure that's safe?" Her expression told him all he needed to know about how good she thought the sushi would be.

"No, it's not airport sushi. This is from Kai's restaurant." He took a portion of eel sushi and let the delicacy flood his senses.

"I've always wondered how good the food was at his place. I've looked it up online, you know?" She started to eat and moaned in happiness. "Holy moly, that's good."

"Right? I'll take you for the fresh from the bar where they make it experience one day."

She smiled, and he could almost hear what she was thinking. If he was right, she was thinking about how much she hated those teppanyaki type places with the open flames, but a sushi chef preparing everything in front of her might be cool. He'd noticed her aversion to flames and electricity, but he'd never make her talk about it. That a fire took away her childhood home and parents was enough of an explanation.

They finished eating over a film that neither one of them really seemed focused on so turned the TV off to go sit on the back deck. It had become a habit over the last few days that if they weren't happy about a film, they'd go out and watch the sun set. It was still hot out, but the nights were getting cooler already, so Roxie grabbed a hoodie from the back of the couch. It was pink and too big for her, but she seemed to like it. It swamped her so much that it was cute.

"Are you going to class at all this week?" Lincoln asked, sliding one of the beers he'd taken from the fridge on his way out over to her.

"The studio decided to cancel my classes for this week to give us all some time to get over Nathan's unplanned visit." She sipped at the beer in a green bottle and put it back down. A few taps of her phone and Lincoln nearly spit his beer out.

"Is that, are you playing *Pink*?" He stressed the singer's name as he stared at her.

"So? *So What* is a good song." She picked up the beer, her left eyebrow raised as she waited for him to answer.

"I guess I just never expected the ballerina to listen to that kind of artist. I'm not judging you, just surprised, that's all." Lincoln wiped at his mouth and took another sip.

"I'll have you know your sister and I loved Pink. Her stuff is good." She winked at him and started to sing along.

Her voice was as beautiful as her face and she had a sound similar to the female rockstar. She got up and started to dance along the deck, not caring who might see her and he thought, not for the first time about how much like Natalie Dormer she looked. It was uncanny but Roxie had the edge on the British actress, her looks were…better. And the way she could move nearly had him begging her to let him take her to bed, but he held back.

She'd let him know when she was ready for that. For now, his alpha-male instincts were appeased. He watched her dance, amazed as always at the grace she displayed with every step, every slither along his deck and back up.

Mandy and Tanya came out, their daughters already upstairs watching TV together.

"You go girl," Mandy said and laughed as she and Tanya joined Roxie in dancing.

Lincoln hadn't quite planned to turn his work family into his home family, but here he was, living with five females and another man because he wanted to keep one of the females completely safe. Not locked away, just safe and always within screaming distance of help.

The ladies all danced for a while, one song blending into another as they enjoyed their night. Lincoln watched, happy to just be near a laughing Roxie.

She finally came and sat down to have a drink from her bottle as the other two women went in to get drinks of their own. "That was fun."

"Nothing like an impromptu dance party, huh?" He asked, pleased to see her cheeks flushed with a smile on her face that nearly lit up the night.

"I love dance of any kind, you know that." She brushed off the question and redid the bun her hair had fallen out of. "That's one reason I've never gone into another field. I could have taken classes and gone into business or nursing, or anything else, but I'm the most alive when I'm dancing."

"I know." He said, his mind on that room where the door remained locked. He checked it every night before he went to bed to make sure. She came alive in that room too, but in a different way than how she lit up when she was dancing.

"What makes you feel like that, Lincoln?" She asked after a long silence. Her face was pointed in his direction, lit up by moonlight and the faint light from the kitchen.

He stared at her, surprised she hadn't figured that

out yet, but if she hadn't, then maybe he should keep it to himself.

"Work, I suppose. My work in Cambodia, for instance. I really enjoy doing things like that. Maybe using a hammer isn't as graceful as a pirouette, but it's something I like doing, building and creating."

"I understand." Her smile was warm, full of surprised pleasure. "Doing something with your body is good for you and it takes some skill to hit a nail and not your own thumb. I know, I've hit my thumb too many times to count."

"Ouch, that does hurt." Lincoln smiled at her, charmed by her admission. "I hope it didn't cause too much damage."

"No, nothing lasting anyway. Want to walk on the beach with me?" Roxie asked suddenly, surprising him.

"What? Yeah, sure. Let me just roll up my pants." He bent to do that and kicked his shoes off. She had shorts on, no shoes, so she was already standing, ready to walk with him.

She'd been a little distant since he made her come and stay with him. After her initial fit of anger, she'd calmed down, but she held herself away from him. That was why it surprised him so much when she slipped her hand into his as they reached the waterline and the surf began to surge and draw sand from beneath their feet.

The wind kicked up, tugging her hair out of the bun

again, but she didn't fix it, she just let her hair whip around her head with a happy smile. She looked as if there was no place else she'd rather be, happy with the warm water from the ocean under her feet and the cool breeze pulling at her hair.

Lincoln let his own body relax as they walked, enjoying the silence and her company. She came up next to him, slipped her arm around his waist and he nearly stopped in shock. Luckily, he saved the moment and slid his own arm around her body.

"This isn't an 'I forgive you' by the way. It's just an 'I'm good with this' kind of thing." She said, her head cradled against his chest.

"I'll take whatever you want to give me, Roxie." He assured her. "I'm not forcing you into anything."

Well, except for that whole picking her up and making her come to his house to live. He refused to feel bad about that, though. Nathan was a shithead who'd hurt her one too many times. Lincoln wanted nothing more than to smash his fist into that punk's nose, but Nathan was in hiding. Or he was if he knew what was good for him.

Maybe telling her to face her problems had been a stupid thing to say that day. Maybe telling her it was safe to go back to her apartment wasn't so smart either. And he had to admit it, he should have been able to explain what had happened with his sister better than he did. He should have made her listen to him that night. From now on, he wasn't going to let her just flounce off in silence without hearing his side of the story, no matter what they might be fighting about.

They both needed to have a say in what happened between them and she was going to have to learn that she didn't know everything, no matter what her experience with men might have been up to now. He was trying to show her he was trustworthy, that he deserved the same respect she demanded. For now, he spent his nights miserable and alone, but it was worth it if it meant she'd come back to his bed a happier woman.

And if she didn't come back to his bed? What then?

He'd simply have to find a way to live with it. He tugged her closer for a second, enjoying what she gave him for now. Later, he'd think about what could, might, happen if she didn't take him back into her bed. Much later.

10

Roxie

oxie's gaze moved around the living room, watching the women that Lincoln somehow managed to invite over without her knowing. He was making too big of a deal out of the whole thing with Nathan showing up at her job, but he was right in some ways. If Nathan had found out where she worked that meant he'd followed her at some point.

And Roxie had to admit that she felt safe now. Over the last few weeks, the days had started to cool off but her coldness to Lincoln had started to thaw. Lincoln had relaxed over time, but he still didn't want her going home. Even if he was the one that had pushed her to do that in the first place.

Roxie tried to hide the way she rolled her eyes at her thoughts and focused on Kitty in the middle of the room showing Keily the one move that would bring any man to his knees. She was at the bottom of a portable pole that Lincoln ordered so that Roxie could practice at home.

"Now what you do is when you get to the bottom and your feet are on the ground, you wrap your arms around the pole, with your head down in front of you. Then you bring your head up like this." Kitty said, whipping her hair behind her head and bringing her eyes up in what was one of the sexiest pouts Roxie had ever seen her pull off.

Wendy, Emily, Keily, and Roxie all clapped and whistled in appreciation of the smoldering looks and the pose Kitty had taken. Kitty pulled herself up with a smile and pranced at the appreciation.

"I definitely want to see you on a proper stage," Keily said to Kitty and sighed. "I really hope this all works out."

"Are you going to have male dancers?" Emily asked, her eyes dancing between Keily and Roxie. "I've begged Dylan to take me to that Magic Mike show, but we haven't been able to catch it anywhere."

Roxie and Keily glanced at each other and laughed.

Roxie decided to answer her perplexed friend. "We had a conversation about that when we first talked about opening a new place. And yes, we want male dancers too."

"I see," Emily said innocently, but Roxie didn't miss the huge grin she tried to hide.

Roxie laughed out loud, really loud, she was so pleased with that grin. She'd laughed so much that evening and it was just perfect. She needed this more than she'd thought. It wasn't her I-have-to-laugh-at-your-awful-joke laugh for clients. It was her real laugh and she'd missed that.

She got up from the couch and wandered over to the pole. There was a song on; *Love is a Bitch* by Two Feet, and it brought out her inner dancer. At first, she swayed, waiting until she caught the rhythm before she started to climb the steel pole. She lost herself in the song, in the moves she twisted through effortlessly.

When she slid down to finish with that move of Kitty's, her eyes caught on Lincoln, not anybody else. The other women were in the room, but Roxie didn't see them. He was standing in the doorway, frozen in place. Something flared to life in her chest and she knew there was a promise in her eyes. One that he'd take her up on later if she let him, his eyes promised back.

He nodded with a faint smile when she pulled her chin up but didn't break from his gaze. Later. Maybe.

There were a lot of maybes in her life lately, but that was okay. For the first time in a while, she had hope for a future with her career, and perhaps something more from Lincoln than either June or she had planned on. Maybe. Lots of maybes. And now she might keep the promise she'd just made.

Later, when everyone had gone home, the PAs were in bed, and Lincoln's driver was wherever he went, Lincoln came into the living room. His walk was casual but there was something predatory in the way his eyes watched her. He was hungry for her, and she couldn't lie - She wanted him.

That song always did something to her and with Lincoln in the house, well, it was inevitable that she'd want him, wasn't it?

"Are you alright?" He asked, watching her closely as she walked over to the pole once more, a song playing softly in the background.

"I'm good, yeah. Thanks for that. I needed a night with my girls." She looked up at him as he walked closer to her and then wrapped his arms around her waist.

She accepted the embrace and wrapped her arms around him. "Happy now?"

"I am." She admitted and surprised herself when she put her head on his chest and relaxed. This was going to happen then.

Her heart started to race as they stood there, just absorbing the heat they each gave off. She took his heat and wasn't surprised when it started to spread throughout her body, rushing to places that soon began to feel as if they would melt if he didn't touch her.

Roxie clutched at his arms, wondering if she should really take this step, but the longer she stared into his brown eyes, the more she wanted to feel every part of him pressed against her. The world around them faded away and there was only her and Lincoln. All she could hear was his breath and hers, their bodies leaning together, wanting so much more.

"Are you sure you want to do this, Roxie?" He whispered the question softly.

"I don't know, Lincoln, but I can't stop it." She paused to lick her hot lips, trying to cool them, but the slick feel of her tongue only made the heat worse. "I want you."

She looked up at him, uncertain, but aching too much to deny herself anymore.

"And I want you too much to convince you that you should go to your room and lock your door. I think I might die if you say no." His eyes were still on hers, that gold streak a warm invitation to fall into him, to let him take care of her worries and do nothing more than please her.

She wanted that, wanted him. "Then take me to your room, Lincoln."

He didn't say anything else. He took her demand as

all the answer she'd give him and turned with her right hand clasped in one of his to take her up the stairs.

He hadn't even kissed her yet, had barely touched her, but Lincoln only had to exist for her to want him. Her body was ready for any touch he gave her, yearning for him to take her clothes off and touch her already. It didn't need to make sense, she didn't have to be certain that this was a good decision, because she wanted him, consequences be damned.

He growled a groan as he closed his bedroom door and pushed her up against it with his hips. The growl vibrated just below her ear, his breath uncontrolled as he inhaled her scent. Roxie leaned her head back, let him lick a hot path from her collarbone up to her ear before his lips slid over to take hers.

She felt him, hard against her lower abdomen, and wanted to feel him in her hand. She pushed the zipper of his trousers down, undid the button to push it all down his waist. He was free and in her hand, hot and throbbing with life.

"Fuck, Roxie. Don't make this end now. Please." He broke the kiss to whisper against her ear. "I love having any part of you wrapped around my dick, but please, let me love you first."

The word love and his plea to let him love her nearly made her gasp, but the gasp escaped into his mouth when he kissed her again. Despite his plea, he moved his hips, pushed himself into her hand until she squeezed him tighter.

Another groan tore from his chest and he pulled away to gently push her to the bed. There was a soft light burning on a dresser, the only light they had to see by, but it was enough as they undressed each other quickly and crawled onto the bed together, their lips still locked.

Lincoln knelt with her on the bed, his breath hot and rapid against her ear now as her hand found him once more.

"Roxie, I want to fuck you until we're both senseless, until I've had enough of you, but I don't think I'll ever have enough." He stroked into her hand, his fingers coming up to tilt her face up to his. He didn't kiss her again, he just looked down into her eyes as he spoke. "I'm going to make you mine again, Roxie. I'm going to make you happy, no matter what I have to do. But if you don't stop, I won't get nearly as far as your eyes are begging me to go."

She smiled, let him go, and sprawled out on the bed. She held her hand out to him, inviting him to join her. "Then do as you please, Lincoln. Tonight, I'm yours."

Lincoln looked down at her, his swimmer's body powerful and displayed perfectly in the faint light. Roxie grinned up at him, totally at ease in her own nudity. Her nipples stood at attention on her chest, ready for his touch. There were no toys, no talk of roles and domination, there were just two young bodies in need of each other.

But it wasn't just that, Roxie knew it. They needed each other, mind and body. That was what made this dangerous. She knew she was giving him a lot more than her body.

Lincoln moved at last, to kneel at her feet. He kissed the skin on the top of her feet, her knees, and then her thighs. His mouth lingered at the skin above her center but moved on, making her body tense up. She'd wanted to feel his tongue there, but maybe later. For now, she'd let him have his way, let him touch what he wanted to touch. There was no rush and she knew he'd go back to give her attention there if she asked, but it didn't matter. She wanted him to do as he pleased, no matter where that meant he'd touch her.

She felt the hot silky touch of his lips against her abdomen and then the tease of his skin against her nipples. He settled on the right one, his tongue stroking out to wet the skin there, to bring it to life. His lips moved, sucked hard at the tender point, drawing a response from more than her breast. Her hips pushed up into his, inviting him to far more than a touch of his lips against her skin.

Lincoln moved his hips to settle his hard length against her in a way that made his movements there slick from her juices. Roxie gasped, wanting him inside of her, but she knew he wasn't done torturing her with pleasure yet. His hand moved to tease her left nipple into life before it moved down to settle onto the spot that ached for his touch, whether it was his tongue or his fingers.

"Let me hear you, Roxie." He asked as he moved his head to her other nipple. "Make those noises I only want to hear from you."

There was an admission there, something she should pay attention to, but it was hard to concentrate when he'd just sparked all her nerve endings to life. She felt her fingers clutch around his biceps, felt the way her hips danced against him, but it was only an awareness of how their bodies moved together, of how good it felt to have him so near to her. Naked and hot against her.

Fuck, her brain was about to unwind, and it didn't matter suddenly. She allowed herself to feel it all, that electric sensation of pure bliss that the stroke of his fingers gave her, and the way his lips around her nipple tugged at something deep inside of her, brought her to a place she didn't know she could get to so quickly. But then, it was Lincoln, and he'd always been able to intuitively give her what she needed. Nobody could make her come faster than he could, even when she wanted it to last.

"Let go, Roxie. Please." His voice urged her, and she couldn't help but do as he asked.

He urged her to ride it out as pulsing waves of pleasure zipped up to her brain and throughout her body. There was no embarrassment, there didn't have to be, there was just bliss and the sensation of Lincoln finally, thank fuck he was finally inside of her.

The pleasure didn't end, it just drifted into a new pleasure, new sensations as he drove into her, pulled back, then dove in all over again. They moved together, their eyes locked now, until Roxie felt the bursts start again, only this time Lincoln followed her. She felt him let go inside of her, the sensation only adding to her own pleasure.

"I'm sorry. I wanted it to last a lot longer than that, but I couldn't, well, control myself." He admitted with a chuckle against her neck before he rolled away to the other side of the bed.

Roxie turned, putting her left leg over his thighs to cradle him. "It's fine. It was perfect. Vanilla but perfect."

"Fuck you, Roxie." He chuckled and sighed, his hot skin a comfort to her. She kissed his hot cheek, and his hot lips, enjoying the sensation.

"Well, I have to admit." She put her head back on the pillow and looked at him with a teasing grin. "Vanilla sex is the best sex when it's with you. It definitely tastes better."

"You..." He growled and pulled her over his body so that she knelt over him. "If I didn't want you so much, I'd send you to your room."

"Oh, does that mean there's going to be a round two?" She teased, licking at his earlobe until he moaned.

"Definitely. And maybe a third or fourth. All vanilla though, we have guests." His hands wrapped around her bottom to push her down against his length. He was hard again already and that was very good.

"I told you, vanilla tastes great when it's with you, Lincoln. Now kiss me before I have to smother you with a pillow to shut you up."

He pulled her head down to his, hiding her grin and smothering her last words. But she didn't mind. Especially when his tongue came out to stroke against hers. It was heaven really.

11

Lincoln

A week had passed since Roxie let him take her back to his bedroom. There were no contracts this time, no demands or promises, just two people that liked making love to each other. Lincoln didn't consider it just sex, or a fuck, it was more with her and always had been.

They were at a café in town, watching the last of the summer people try to frolic in water that was already turning cold. All the kids were back in school, so this was the last of the summer people, those that chose to take later dates to get better deals on resorts or were lower on the ladder at work. "What's it like here in the winter?" He asked.

"It's quieter." She answered, her eyes on two seagulls

fighting over a sandwich wrapper not far away. "I love summer, but I do like the calm that settles over the place in the fall and winter months."

"You get the beach back and all the parking spaces?" He asked with a soft laugh.

"Exactly. And I can just walk into a salon to get my nails done, none of this appointment bullshit that I hate." She took a sip of her coffee and leaned back in the white wooden fold-out chair that matched the others around six tables in front of the café.

Lincoln was about to answer when his phone buzzed. He saw it was Kai and picked up immediately.

"Hey, Lincoln. Got some bad news, pal. Nathan's been sniffing around your house." Kai said before Lincoln could speak.

"Um, and nobody did anything about it?" Lincoln's jaw went rigid and he glanced at the people around them. No sign of that moron.

"What's wrong?" Roxie asked and leaned forward to look at him.

"Just a minute, Rox." He smiled to reassure her and spoke again. "So, what happened?"

"He spotted one of my new hires and took off," Kai replied and Lincoln could almost hear him shrugging. Kai was that predictable.

"Good. He knows not to fuck around then. Thanks for letting me know, Kai." Lincoln said into the phone and glanced over at Roxie again. She looked a little miffed. Damn.

"Sorry." He said once he'd hung up. "Nathan's been at the house, or near it. Listen."

He paused to point out people sitting at other tables or walking near the other shops around them. "You see that woman? With the floppy hat? She works for Kai. That man with the socks and the sandals? Also works for Kai. They're here to protect you from him."

"Okay?" Roxie looked around, her eyes wide in surprise. "We're surrounded by security people?"

"Yes, and you have been for a while. I didn't have enough at the studio that night he attacked you, but I do now. I got Kai to hire more."

"Wow. So, wait, Kai runs a security agency or something too?" She asked, her eyes back on him. The white crocheted top she wore, perfect for the cooler air today, set off the blue of her eyes.

"They work in the background for him, and by extension, me. I'm paying him for their time and expenses. They look like everyday people, but they're all trained to protect you. Some will be martial arts experts, others some other form of training, but all of them are armed."

"You're paying them?" Fuck, he had more money than she thought then. Wow. "Okay, so explain why Kai has so many security experts around please."

"At first, it was so we could all lead as normal a life as possible, but him especially. Apparently, he was kidnapped when he was very young and he's been living surrounded by other people like this since his parents got him back. There was one time, when we were together at university, that I got really freaked out because I thought this guy was stalking me. Turns out Kai just had him following me to keep an eye on me. I've grown used to it now, but that really freaked me out."

"Kai was kidnapped as a child? How come you never told me that? What happened? Poor guy." Roxie's face twisted with concern and that just made Lincoln's heart melt a little. She was such a good friend to those around her that learning about this hurt her.

"Well, I didn't tell you because I don't know much about what happened. Kai never talks about it and that's all I know; that he was kidnapped but his parents got him back. He's very private about it all and always hypervigilant about it. I don't know if it was just that so many Chinese boys got kidnapped back then or if his family was targeted because they were rich, but yeah, that happened.

"Uh, what do you mean so many Chinese boys were kidnapped back then?" Roxie looked deeply worried, and he rushed to answer her.

"It was to do with that one-child policy that they had. If parents couldn't have boys, they'd pay for one.

Sometimes girls would go missing but boys were seen as the future, as they carry on the family name and are valued over girls." He'd already decided to not talk about the shadier side of all of that because she looked so troubled about it.

"It's all so despicable. So many children go missing every year around the world. It's horrifying." She shuddered and looked out at the people around them. "I'm glad Kai went back to his family."

"It explains a lot about the guy, I guess. Knowing that happened to him changed a lot about the world for me. He explained to me how this one woman kidnapped over a thousand children by feeding them drugged treats. She'd walk along with this sleepy kid by her side, and nobody ever questioned it. She got away with it for years." Lincoln paused, not wanting to go on, but he'd started now. "She was selling them on to people that would sell them again to people that wanted boys for field workers, whatever they were needed for."

"I don't want to think about it, but I can't help it when I hear stories like that. I know a lot of bad stuff happens in my line of work, but at least I'm an adult. I have a chance of protecting myself. Kids don't." Roxie sighed and Lincoln couldn't help but feel bad about ruining their afternoon out.

"I'm sorry. I didn't want to make you sad, I just wanted to be honest with you." He took her hand and she smiled at him, though it wasn't one of her brightest smiles to date.

"I know. Thank you. Can we go home? I don't want to be out here anymore. I just feel like a target." She shuddered and pushed down the sleeves of her top to hide her arms. "I'm cold now too."

"Let's get you back home. I'll have Kai put more men around the house."

"I don't know whether to be flattered or worried that you're a creepy stalker, having all of these people watching me." She said once they were back at her car. "I mean, it's really sweet, but at the same time…come on, Lincoln. Are you a creep?"

He was happy that she was back to teasing him and sent her a playful frown as he buckled his seatbelt. "I'm totally stalking you, babe."

"I don't blame you. I'm totally stalkable." She started the engine, and they were off. "Although, it's weirding me out that you had people around me all this time, that other people I trust have paid people to watch me all this time and I never suspected a thing."

He was definitely not going to tell her about Tanya and Mandy watching her old apartment then. Nope, keeping that all to himself, he decided.

"It's only because Kai and I care about you, Roxie. It wasn't to control your movements or anything." He said in total seriousness. "Nathan is unstable, unpredictable, and that's dangerous."

"I know, Lincoln, I just..." She paused at a stoplight and glanced over at him. "I'll get used to it I guess."

"I hope you won't have to. If the cops do their job, or Kai's people for that matter, then he'll be in prison and won't be a problem anymore." Lincoln left the 'I hope' unspoken. Nathan, or the people he owed money to, could still be a problem.

"We'll see," Roxie said, distracted by the afternoon traffic. She got them home safely and Lincoln looked around.

He spotted a dozen people around his property line, all dressed in black cargo shorts, black t-shirts, with heavy-duty boots on their feet. They didn't appear to be armed but Lincoln had no doubt they were. Good.

He went in and started to make dinner for them both. She'd wanted his version of a vegetarian casserole when they went out so that was what he'd decided to make. She went up to change into a pink long-sleeved t-shirt and pink yoga pants that did wonderful things to her ass. He grinned as she walked in and washed her hands. "What are you doing?"

"I'm going to make those cheese things with the crescent rolls to go with the casserole." She smiled and started to take the things she needed out of the fridge.

"Hmm. That's not very vegetarian, all that cheese."

"I don't care what it is, asshole." She teased back with eyes she blinked angelically. "I'm making it."

"You go girl." He replied and went back to slicing up squash and zucchini. "You make that cheese thing all you want."

"I am, thank you." She started to mix ingredients but paused, her eyes on the windows. He looked up with her and saw one of the women working the security detail. "Reckon they're hungry too?"

"Are you telling me you want to feed all of them too?" He asked, knowing that's exactly what she was thinking.

"Maybe." She went and got more ingredients out of the fridge. "Here's more vegetables."

"Eating will distract them." He told her but she just shook her head. "No, it won't. They look like professionals. They won't be distracted."

"Fine, rinse that squash off for me, please." He sighed, shaking his head. It was one more thing to appreciate about Roxie. She had a kind heart.

"What about Tanya, Mandy, and the girls?" She asked but he had the answer to that.

"They, including my driver, have gone out to the movies and are going out to eat after."

"Oh. Wait. So, you're telling me we've had the house to ourselves all this time and you didn't tell me?" She paused, looking up at him with a look of disbelief.

"Yeah, why?" He wasn't sure why that was a problem.

"The room, Lincoln! We could have been in the playroom instead of at that café." She smiled, but there was still disbelief on her face. "You didn't want to use that time for that?"

"Oh, um, well, I thought you'd want to avoid that place for a while. Until we were on better footing." He shrugged, trying not to look worried, but smugly nonchalant. He wasn't sure he pulled it off.

"Oh." She answered, staring at a block of cream cheese. "Does that mean you don't want to use the room with me anymore?"

"No, not at all." He glanced up to reassure her with a smile. "I'm just enjoying what we're doing now. Don't worry, when we get back to that room, we're going to tear it apart using everything in there until it breaks."

"Oh." She said again, but this time her cheeks were pink. He wasn't sure if that was because she was pleased or because his words aroused her. Knowing Roxie, it was probably both. "Good, you don't want to use it with anyone else then."

"Um, no. Also, I'm fairly certain you'd padlock my dick if I even tried."

"You never know." She was the one going for smug nonchalance this time but on her, it was way hotter than it was on him. "I might like to watch."

"I seriously doubt that." He spit out, looking at her.

He wasn't so sure she was kidding but wasn't sure he was ready for her answer, so he didn't push for one.

"I might." She repeated with a grin. "I'm never going to be totally vanilla you know?"

"I fucking hope not." He leaned over to kiss her cheek before he spoke again. "I would miss that side of you if you woke up one day completely tame. I'd hate seeing you demand nothing more than the missionary position. Especially after the way you moved your ass against me this morning."

He lost himself in the memory of her pressed up against his bedroom door, taking every one of his strokes with a quiet gasp that brought his dick to life all over again just thinking about it. He had to pause his slicing to let that problem go away before he could start again.

"That was fun, but it's hardly kinky." She groused at him in mock disapproval.

"There were people in the house who would not have approved. Totally different from that party you threw here." He reminded her of the housewarming party that she'd thrown for him.

"Still not kinky." She shook her head and started to stir the mixture she'd put on top of the crescent rolls then fold up to bake in the oven. "Now, if you'd taken me to the room without any of them noticing and tied me to the wall, that would have been kinky."

"Don't tempt me, woman, there's still nobody home." He shook the keys to the door to let her know he had them.

"Oh, promises, promises." She fluttered her eyelashes with a smirk that ruined the innocent look.

"Bitch." He growled at her, but it only made her grin wider.

"I know. Do you need oil for that?" She pointed but it didn't look like she was pointing at the bowl he was dropping the vegetables into. It looked like she was pointing at something below his waist.

"What?" He asked, wondering where she was going with her question.

"The casserole? Have you added oil yet?" She smirked again, walked up to him, and put her index finger on his bottom lip. "Or, I might have been asking if you want me to oil up your dick so we can figure out where else you can put it? Choice is yours."

"Tease. I'm making dinner for all those people out there now that you made that decision and you know it. But later we're going to find out a lot more about that last part. I promise." And he meant it.

12

Roxie

"Time to wake up, Roxie." A voice intruded into her dreams, and she smiled without opening her eyes. She knew that voice.

"Good morning to you too, Lincoln." She opened her eyes at last and saw Lincoln standing at the side of the bed, a tray in his hands. "Breakfast in bed?"

"Not just any breakfast in bed, *birthday* breakfast in bed." He set the tray down once she'd slid up against the pillows.

"You remembered my birthday?" She stared up at him, touched that he'd remembered her real birthday.

"Of course. Why wouldn't I?" He took the extra glass of orange juice from the tray and had a sip before he spoke again. "You're 28 today, even though everyone you know here still thinks you're 26."

She blushed when he mentioned the lie she'd told all those years ago. It had been a silly thing, a lie to keep her from opening a bank account to deposit checks more than anything. Back then, she wanted to be paid in cash and employers didn't like to pay people underage working in strip clubs with checks. So, she'd lied about her age.

"I thought I explained that." She told him, not certain now.

"It was about being paid in cash, wasn't it?" He sat down and watched her, not saying anything else.

"Yes, that's it." She picked up her fork, pleased that he'd made her pancakes. And if she wasn't mistaken, he'd made her most favorite pancakes in the world. Her first bite after pouring maple syrup all over the stack of fluffy, golden pancakes told her she was right. "Damn, you're after my heart! You made these just like Mr. Parker used to."

"Well, we'll talk about that later." Lincoln winked at her, and she knew there was something more, but he wasn't ready to reveal what yet. "I have a full day planned with you, so I hope you don't have other plans?"

"Nope, I don't work on my real birthday, even if people don't know about it, so I have no plans at all." She took her last bite and put the fork down. "Those were amazing, and I haven't tasted anything like them in ten years. Thank you."

He took the kiss on the cheek she offered as she got up to dress. "Wear something…nice. Comfortable but nice."

"Hm, where are you taking me?" She went to the door and looked back at him.

"Somewhere special. We have to take a short flight to get there, so hurry." He stood up, went to his own closet, and began to take his clothes off to change.

Excitement made her ignore how good he looked without his clothes on, even if he was drop-dead gorgeous. What did he have planned for her now?

It had been a week since that day Nathan was seen near the house and he hadn't been seen since. She wasn't completely relaxed now, but she wasn't as on edge as she had been. Lincoln would keep her safe.

She looked through her closet, found a dark blue, flounce-sleeve Stella McCartney dress she'd bought online from a shop she trusted with her hard-earned cash. The hemline hit her mid-thigh, but Lincoln would appreciate the look. She pulled a pair of black heels to wear with the dress, a white knit cardigan in case she got cold later, and showered before dressing quickly.

Once she was dressed, with some light makeup on, she twisted her hair up in a sophisticated knot and put her shoes on. Just as she was walking down the stairs she caught a familiar smell. It smelled just like the diner where Mr. Parker made his delicious pancakes. Did Lincoln figure out the recipe or something?

Puzzled, she walked into the kitchen to find the last person she expected, Mr. Parker. He was older now, of course, with more gray in his hair than black, but it was him. "Mr. Parker?"

"Hiya, Chloe! How you doing, babes? Come give me a hug. I haven't seen you in forever." He held his arms out to her and Roxie immediately walked into the tall, very round man's arms.

"What are you doing here?" She asked as she stepped back.

"Making you birthday pancakes. Oh, and this." Mr. Parker turned to the fridge and opened the freezer door. He pulled out a tall glass filled with what she suspected was her favorite milkshake, another treat Mr. Parker used to make.

"Is that...?" She pointed at the glass, too stunned to say anything else.

"A pineapple milkshake? You know it is, babes. Come on, sit down and enjoy it before the rest of Lincoln's bunch come down for their breakfast." He waved at the table across from where he was cooking.

Roxie sat down, feeling for the first time in ages like the Chloe she used to be. With the first tug at the straw, her mouth filled with pineapple goodness and she moaned in pleasure. The pancakes were heavenly, the best in the world, with vanilla being Mr. Parker's secret ingredient. But add in the milkshake and this might be the best birthday ever.

"Happy birthday, by the way, Chloe. I hope you've had a good day so far?" Mr. Parker flipped over another stack of pancakes as he waited for her to answer. Her eyes fixed on the delicious stack and she decided that she would have some more later.

"Oh yes, heavenly really." She smiled a smile full of innocent pleasure. "I guess Lincoln brought you down here?"

"He did yes, and I'm glad he did. I always wondered what happened to you." His round, red face was full of concern.

"It's a long story, but I survived it all." She went back to her milkshake just as Lincoln came in.

"You're good with my driver taking you back to the airport?" Lincoln asked Mr. Parker.

Mr. Parker wiped his hands down his chef's whites and nodded. "Yep, I'm all done."

"Good, he's here. But I can drop you off if you prefer? We're off on a little trip of our own."

"Nah, Lincoln, I don't want to intrude. I'll see you soon, though, right?" Mr. Parker held a hand out in question.

"As soon as I get back to New York you know I'll be

there." Lincoln shook Mr. Parker's hand and then turned to Roxie. "Ready?"

"Yeah, let me just say goodbye once more."

Roxie hugged the man and told him goodbye before she turned to Lincoln. "I'm ready."

"I hope you are." Lincoln grinned and led her out to the car. "You look good by the way."

"Thanks, so do you." She replied, noting that Lincoln was in his normal Brioni suit.

"That's very kind of you." He replied smoothly, but she saw the smirk on his face.

"Dick." She muttered but he heard her.

"I have one, yes. And I love how you take it." He said with a cheeky wink as he got into the driver's seat.

"You asshole. I still hate you, you know?" She asked, her left eyebrow lifted in challenge.

"I know. I still hate you too." He started the engine and Roxie turned to him, a question on her lips.

"How is the driver going to take Mr. Parker back?" She asked, worried the man might miss his flight.

"He's going to use Mandy's car." Lincoln moved the car around traffic and soon had them headed for the airport.

"Where are we going?" She finally asked, wondering because he hadn't told her to pack anything.

"To a little place in Charlotte, North Carolina. You'll

like it." Lincoln didn't turn his head away from traffic as he drove along.

It was a short drive to the airport and soon enough they were in the air.

The plane was a Beechcraft King Air 350 that belonged to Kai, according to Lincoln. Roxie noted the pilots closed the wood panel doors to the cockpit after a brief chat with Lincoln before they took off.

"Everything alright?" She asked once they were in the air and cruising along.

"Fine, really." Lincoln uncoupled his seatbelt and came to kneel in front of her. "How are you?"

"I'm good. What are you doing?" She asked, an intrigued smile letting him know she was open to anything.

"I'm telling you happy birthday again." He answered smoothly as he used the palms of his hands to spread her knees apart. His head came down to tease at her neck, pulling a throaty chuckle from her.

"Like that is it?" She asked with a hitch in her voice, excitement already flooding through her.

"Definitely," Lincoln said softly as he pulled her hips out a little then pushed up the hem of her dress. "You won't need these for now."

He pulled down the black lace and satin panties she wore before he stuffed the undergarment in the pocket of his pants. Once he had her exactly where he wanted her, his head came down to kiss her right thigh, then the left. "You are beautiful, Roxie and you deserve a lifetime of birthdays just like this."

His fingers retraced the steps his lips took as they traveled up her thighs and then up to her center. Roxie forgot how to breathe the moment his tongue found the perfect spot, her fingers gripped into the supple leather armrests. Everything in the plane was white but Roxie didn't care about that, not when he slipped a finger inside of her.

It occurred to her that he hadn't undressed her, except for her panties. He hadn't touched her anywhere above her waist, he'd only touched what was below. It didn't matter though, her breath still caught in her chest as his lips sucked at the button that seemed to contain a million nerve endings, each one sending a burst of pleasure through different parts of her body.

Roxie's eyes fluttered open for a moment and she looked out of the window at the fluffy clouds outside with a sultry smile. Another new experience with Lincoln. She ground her hips down, tilting at just the right angle to make the pleasure flow through more of her body. She knew very well that sex wasn't just about the end goal, it was about enjoying the parts in between. And right now, she was enjoying every moment.

Her tongue darted out to wet dry lips while her hands moved to her nipples, cupping them through the thin fabric of her dress and bra. Lincoln glanced up and gave her a wink of approval as her fingers closed on her nipples. That look told her to go ahead, do what she wanted. But that only created an urge to touch him.

Her left hand slid down her body to reach for his mouth then slipped up his cheek and into his hair. Without thinking about it, her right leg came up in the seat to open herself more to him, her fingers gripped in his hair to hold his head in place. Roxie's hips danced to the tune of his tongue and the two fingers he now used to tease her higher.

She groaned softly, not certain how much the pilots up front would hear. He gave an answering groan, a sound full of need, but he didn't move. He must be aching to fuck her by now, but it was her birthday and he'd said this day was about her. She would worry about what *she* wanted right now.

Roxie stopped thinking again when everything came together at just the right pace, when her breath caught in her chest. She took in gasps of air, not aware of the way she moaned his name over and over. All she knew was Lincoln's scent, her own scent, and the way he made her feel.

Loved and pleasured, sensations she wasn't used to at all, Roxie finally let go. Her fingers clawed deeper into his hair, her back arched, and everything became a blur, a blank place where all that existed was what Lincoln made her feel. She didn't want to leave that place, she didn't want to go back to the real world, not when this place gave her so much bliss.

She was aware of the way Lincoln touched her, of how his tongue never stopped stroking her, or how he never stopped loving her. Shit.

Did he love her? Is that what all of this meant? She wondered, as he pulled away to wipe his face with a napkin. He put the napkin in the pocket of his suit jacket, revealing a pleased smirk.

Damn, even when he smirked, he was sexy.

But even that thought didn't distract her from that fleeting question she'd had. Did Lincoln love her?

She thought back over the last few months, of the things he said when he wasn't paying attention or that he thought wouldn't reveal anything. He'd been looking for her since that night ten years ago. Why?

Surely, he hadn't loved her back then? She'd been infatuated with his brother anyway, so maybe she didn't notice. She'd also hated his guts, but that was beside the point. Or had that one night they'd spent together really changed him?

Or had he come to love her over the last few months? If he'd loved her back then he'd been in love with a spoiled little girl who didn't know what life was about at all. Naïve and overprotected, that's what she'd been, but she soon learned how to take care of herself.

Now Lincoln was back in her life, caring for her, taking care of her, and insisting that she be as cocooned from the world as she'd once been by her parents. Was that love?

After her experiences with Nathan, she didn't want to be in love. He'd fooled her, hurt her, scarred her emotionally. Her infatuation all those years ago with Liam hadn't been real when it came down to it. They'd exchanged secret love notes, but never had conversations together. Not private ones, anyway.

There'd been men in her life between Lincoln and Nathan, but those had mainly been arrangements she'd made with rich men to make sure she could eat and have a place to call home. There'd definitely been no love in those relationships.

Which left her questioning why she was here now. She'd let Lincoln take her to his place, without another contract, without a promise of anything. Was that because she loved him? That was a worrying thought, but she couldn't push it away. Did she love this man who seemed to want to make the world hers?

She watched him get back into his chair, buckle up, and take her left hand in his. She stared at their joined hands, wondering if she was in far more trouble than she'd originally thought?

13

Roxie

They left the plane behind and were soon in a limo. The car pulled up to a mall and Roxie couldn't help but wonder. "You brought me here to go to the mall?"

"Kind of." Lincoln grinned, waggling his eyebrows at her. "There's a specific store here. I could have taken you back to New York, but I want to get back to the house before lunch."

It was only 9:30 am and the flight was less than an hour, so they weren't going to be here long. He walked her through the mall and then she saw the store that his eyes were focused on. "Lincoln? Tiffany's?"

"Yes, Roxie. Stop dragging your feet. Come on. Let

me spoil you." He tugged at her hand, and she followed him quickly.

Oh boy. She and June thought he was incapable of love, but he might just be about to prove them wrong. What was he about to do?

"Hello, Mr. Young, I'm Ana. I'm so glad you're here." An older blonde woman dressed in a black business suit with a white blouse came up to greet them. "Would you like coffee or another drink?"

"I don't, thank you. Roxie?" He looked at her, but she was speechless and just shook her head.

He was not about to give her an engagement ring, was he? Men had never taken her to a jewelry store. If they bought her things, they brought the pieces to her. And Tiffany's? Wasn't that where all the women dreamed of getting an engagement ring from?

"Very good, follow me please." The woman smiled at them both and turned to take them to a room in the back. "This is your order, Mr. Young. I hope it meets your approval."

There on a table sat a wide box and a much smaller ring box. Both were open and Roxie's heart started to beat again when she saw the ring wasn't an engagement ring at all. It was a firefly ring with a huge tanzanite centerpiece, surrounded with round diamonds set in platinum. It was the most precious thing she'd ever seen. Then she saw the bangle in the wider Tiffany blue box.

It was just like one her parents bought her when she was sixteen. There were five silver bands in the one her parents bought her but this one had an extra band encrusted with small diamonds.

"Lincoln?" She asked as he pulled out a seat for her.

"I know, it's not exactly the same as the one your parents got you all those years ago on your Sweet Sixteen, but I hope this brings you some happiness."

"It's beautiful." She picked up the bangle and slid it over her wrist, ignoring the price tag still attached for all she was worth.

"I can't give you that bangle back, but I hope we can start over with a new Tiffany bracelet. And the ring. The way the diamonds sparkle reminded me of your eyes too much to say no to it." Lincoln spoke to Roxie, but he nodded to the saleswoman.

The woman cut the price tag off the bangle and the ring before she slid the ring onto the third finger of Roxie's right hand.

"It's beautiful Lincoln, wow. I'm so...." There were tears in her eyes and she had to blink them away before she leaned over to hug him. "Thank you, I love them both."

"Good." He said, his own voice a little thick. He handed the woman a credit card and she quickly came back with a receipt.

Roxie tried to look away, but she caught something

that looked like it said he'd paid over $4000 for her gifts. She tried not to think about that and looked at the ring and bangle now resting on her right hand and wrist. She smiled as the light in the dark room caught the shine of the diamonds. "I'm going to need a bodyguard to make sure I don't get mugged." She said jokingly.

"You've got me to protect you and we'll be back home soon enough. Thank you, Ana, wonderful doing business with you."

"Thank you, Mr. Young. Enjoy your birthday, ma'am." The woman gave a curt nod before they walked out of the shop with two boxes in a small blue bag.

The drive back to the plane was silent as Lincoln answered text messages and emails. He was reading a report as they took off back to Myrtle Beach. She kept looking at the gifts he'd given her, enjoying the way they caught the light. But she spent more time watching him than she did anything. He was always a fascinating man, but now?

She had to add sweet and considerate to the list of hidden qualities Lincoln had. Trust him to remember a gift she'd been given twelve years ago by her parents. Had he been at that party? She vaguely remembered seeing him around the edges of the ballroom her parents rented to throw the massive party in. Now that she thought about it, she even remembered a sweet, chaste kiss on her cheek as he handed her a small gift wrapped in a box.

There'd been a pair of tickets to see one of her favorite bands inside the box. She'd gone with June, of course. Had she even thanked him for that gift? She had when he handed her the box, but that had been it. Had Lincoln always been this sweet and she'd just been too stupid to see it?

For a moment she wondered if she was part of the reason he didn't believe in love. If he had been in love with her back then, and she'd run off after the night he'd whisked her away from danger, maybe she was. But surely, he hadn't loved the silly girl she was back then?

"We're about to land. Are you alright?" He brought her out of her thoughts, and she couldn't help but smile at him.

"I'm fine, Lincoln. I'm not fine china, you know?" He'd treated her like porcelain since Nathan assaulted her at the studio. It was a little smothering, but she knew he couldn't help it.

He did care about her, she knew that. If he didn't, he wouldn't be so kind and generous to her. But love? She watched his face as he settled back into the seat, wondering all over again.

She put her thoughts away as they left the airport behind and he drove them back to the house. She had to answer text messages from so many people she wondered why she'd become suddenly popular. Emily asked her if she wanted a Versace dress she didn't want anymore. Kitty wanted to know where Roxie got an outfit she'd worn at a gig a few months back. Wendy wanted to know which hair straightener Roxie used. Mandy wanted to know if she could sign up for Roxie's class.

"Why has everybody suddenly decided they need to talk to me today?" Roxie asked, putting her phone down as soon as they walked into the house.

"I have no idea, but that's how it goes, isn't it? You'll go weeks sometimes with nothing, then all of sudden everybody needs your attention. I need yours now by the way." He said, taking her hand to take her upstairs. He walked down the hallway to a room that they'd left empty from the beginning. Lincoln said he didn't know what he wanted to do with it.

Was it another playroom? Everyone was out for the day, the kids at school, and Mandy and Tanya were gone as well. Did he want to play? She was up for that if he was.

Instead of a room filled with sex toys, she walked into one with a mirrored wall and a barre in place. The walls were painted a soft shade of blue with lots of room for her to practice in, even with the grand piano in one corner. It wasn't exactly the same as her old studio, but it was close.

"I had this installed as well," Lincoln said, moving to a side wall and pressing into it. A hidden door opened, and Roxie walked over to find drawers filled with ballet costumes, shoes, and even a few tutus hanging from a rod.

"That's incredible, Lincoln." She said with a hug as he came up to stand beside her.

"I know I can't replace your old studio, or the people you've lost along the way, and I can't take away your pain, but I hope this reminds you of the good times from the past, helps you to remember the past with more joy."

"I don't know what to say, Lincoln." She looked up at him, at a loss for words. "Thank you."

"Why don't you hit play on that?" Lincoln pointed at a small stand that held a stereo.

The thing was old, and she grew certain as she got up next to it that it was exactly like the one she had in her studio all those years ago.

"Turn it on," Lincoln said as she looked over the stereo, putting her fingers on familiar buttons.

Roxie flipped a button without looking and her finger automatically found the play button for the CD player. A familiar thump started, and Roxie covered her mouth, her eyes wide. "Are you serious?"

Don't Cha by the Pussycat Dolls filled the room and Roxie began to dance as memories flooded her mind.

She and June used to dance to this all the time, out of the prying eyes of their parents, daring each other into dirtier versions of each routine they came up with. Her body remembered the steps and she gave Lincoln his own private performance.

He went to the wardrobe, took out a black tutu, and held it from one finger as she came to a stop in front of him. She took off the dress she'd worn, kicked off her shoes, and put the tutu on to continue dancing for him.

"I've always wanted to fuck you in one of those." He growled, but she slithered away from him, combining exotic dancing and ballet.

She ignored what he'd just revealed about how long he'd wanted her and danced over to the piano as the song ended. She tapped the black piano with her eyebrows raised.

"At your service, ma'am." He drawled. "What would you like me to play?"

"Hmm, *Ave Maria*?" She asked, tapping her chin.

"Indeed." He answered with a crack of his knuckles.

He walked over, enjoying the sight of her in a black bra and panties with a black tutu over, if the look on his face meant anything. Sheer joy spread over her face as he began to play, and her feet, legs, and arms began to move.

He didn't sing the vocal parts, but he didn't need to. She could hear them in her head. It was beautiful to dance, though she didn't have her ballet slippers on, in such a private, beautiful studio again. She lost herself in the steps, letting her body move with ease from one position to the next with a grace she'd never lost.

The last note rang in the air, vibrating from the piano as Lincoln's fingers stilled and he stood up. Her gaze caught his and she'd never seen such desire on his face. Her breath caught in her chest as he stalked over to pick her up and carry her to the room she hadn't been in for a very long time.

Lincoln clasped her wrists in the handcuffs at the top of the table and she waited, her body on fire for whatever it was he planned. Desire surged into her veins as he pulled her bra cups down and attached small metal clamps to each nipple. The skin burned, surged with sparks of pleasure that were only surpassed by the pleasure she found when he pulled her panties down and attached a suction cup to her clit. He was quick about his work, performing each task with skill before he finally stood over her, staring down at her with a roguish smile.

"You're going to come so hard you'll think you've died and gone to heaven." He said just before he put a blindfold over her eyes. Then it seemed he walked away because she did not feel his touch at all.

Headphones went over her ears, and she heard Two Feet singing that song that made her shiver with need.

He'd watched her dance to that song not long ago. He'd stared at her in stark desire and now, with every drag of a baseline that echoed around in her ears, she twisted her hips. That bass was hypnotic, and the pulses of each new sound timed with the pleasure circling around her body.

She jumped when she felt his lips on her arm. Her head followed his when his tongue traced the swell of her breasts. His fingers dancing on her thighs made her legs draw together in a tight clench as she bit her lip. Her toes curled so far against her feet that she felt the joints pop. She didn't care, she just wanted his touch.

The song changed.

I Feel Like I'm Drowning came on next and in that totally dark place, she actually listened to the song. Kind of. She did feel like she was drowning. And yeah, Lincoln was holding her down, but no, he wasn't killing her. Well, he kind of was. With pleasure.

The table moved and she realized he'd climbed onto it. Her legs wrapped around his hips and she smiled up at him, blind and deaf but for the song playing in her head.

Lincoln's hand came up to delve into her folds as a new song came on. Another one from the same guy, that she didn't know, but the words mattered. The singer didn't want anybody else, was that what Lincoln was telling her?

She had to wonder if he was hearing the same song because Lincoln thrust into her just as the bass kicked in. "Fuck."

She didn't know if she screamed it or moaned it, but she wasn't really in a position to care. Her body was on fire, even her head might be.

She braced herself when he took the clamps off her nipples, knowing that the blood would surge back in and make her head pop off. But no amount of bracing could have prepared her for the tingling explosion that tore through her body as he thrust into her in time with the song.

She stopped listening to words, she just felt, as her body arched on the table, her feet braced against the length of Lincoln's back. He didn't let go of her, he didn't lose his pace, he just fucked, and it was so damn good.

His fingers dug into her hips to hold her still, to stop the writhing twist of her hips, as he made one final thrust that shook her. Those fingers dug tighter, deliciously tighter, as he pulsed inside of her. Roxie waited, trying to catch her breath as he lost himself in her.

He sank back eventually, withdrawing from her.

She felt the suction cup disappear, then the headphones and blindfold were taken away. She looked at him, seeing how shaken he was. She looked down to see she still wore the tutu. Roxie smiled, looking up at him.

"Was it as good as you fantasized about?" Her tone was teasing, but his eyes were still on fire.

"Better. But then, reality is always better than anything I fantasize about when it comes to you."

He released her wrists and she got up from the table to find her legs had turned to jelly.

"Let me help you get a shower." He whispered against her head as he carried her to their private bathroom. "There's more to come."

14

Roxie

"You mean Kai owns this place too?" Roxie looked at one of the most exclusive restaurants in Myrtle Beach.

"Yeah, he's got a thing for restaurants," Lincoln said as he handed the keys to a parking attendant and came to take her arm. "I've not told them it's your birthday, but I've invited a few friends to dinner."

"Oh?" She asked, her heart thudding in her chest. Would the ones that didn't know her real birthday figure it out? How would she ever explain all the lies she'd told to protect herself, to hide her real identity over the years?

The restaurant was perfect, with lots of glass walls to look out at the ocean, white tablecloth-covered tables, and black chairs. They were led to the edge of the restaurant next to the glass wall, where a huge round table took up space.

It seemed they were the last to arrive as there were only two chairs empty.

"Are we late?" She whispered to Lincoln.

"A little. I wasn't planning for round two in the shower." He whispered back.

Everybody waved as they finally sat down. June was to her right and Roxie leaned over to kiss her cheek hello.

"Happy birthday, my sweet friend. Your secrets are safe with me." June whispered to her before Roxie pulled back.

"Thank you." Roxie mouthed the words and looked around the table to greet everybody. Emily was there with Dylan. Keily had brought her husband Logan who was fucking gorgeous, just as Keily described him. Kitty, with River at her side, waved over to them and Roxie waved back.

Kai was on the other side of June and Wendy was on Kitty's other side. Lincoln had said her favorite people would be here and he was right. There was one of Lincoln's old friends too, Trevon, who still reminded Roxie of that duke from the regency Netflix series.

"Um, I know we weren't supposed to, Lincoln told me not to, but I got you a present," June said quietly, once Roxie had greeted everyone and ordered a glass of red wine.

"What?" Roxie asked and looked down. June handed over a Louis Vuitton handbag and Roxie opened it to find the bag full of Dior lipsticks. Roxie looked over at June with her mouth hanging open in surprise.

"I couldn't remember which one was your favorite, so I got them all. I'm sure you can pull them all off, but if there's some you don't like just give them away or something." June said with a pleased smile.

"You're too generous, June," Roxie growled at her with wide eyes, but she couldn't stop smiling at the memory those tubes invoked.

"Anything for you, baby. Anything." June said and patted her hand.

"If I could steal her for a moment, dear sister?" Lincoln asked, leaning around Roxie.

"Sure." June smiled at her brother, but her eyes were on Roxie, telling her she knew there was more between Roxie and Lincoln all along. Roxie gave a guilty shrug and turned to Lincoln.

"What's up?" Roxie asked him with a happy smile. She was as carefree as she'd ever been before the worst day of her life changed everything. Nothing could mar this night for her.

"Well, it's just that there's cake for after dinner. Do

you want to tell everybody it's your real birthday or not?"

Roxie looked at him sharply, before her eyes drifted around the table. These people were all her friends and would forgive her the little lie, wouldn't they? She looked back at him, worry making her frown.

"I think they'll understand, Roxie. I really do." He patted her thigh to reassure her, and she looked back out at her friends.

"Uh, if everyone could give me their attention for a moment? I have something to explain that may upset some of you. But please, let me get to the end and if you are upset with me, well, I'll understand." She paused to see that she had everyone's eyes and continued. "Ten years ago, my parents died. I was known as Chloe up to that point. I was eighteen years old the night our house suspiciously caught fire. I ran, due to circumstances that told me I should run far, far away, and well, I ended up here, as Roxie. And, um, today's my real birthday."

There was silence around the table. Her friends looked at her and it was Kitty that spoke first. "What the fuck, Roxie?"

"I'm sorry, Kitty. Really, I am."

"What the hell do you mean it's your birthday? I didn't get you a gift!" Kitty glared at her but then smiled. "No need to explain, honey, really. We all have our secrets and stories to tell, don't we?"

Kitty looked around the table and everyone seemed to agree. Roxie saw love and acceptance in their faces. Relief made her head swim for a minute, but she took a deep breath.

"So, uh, do you still want us to call you Roxie?" June asked, her brown eyes smiling happily.

"Yes, please. I've become used to it," Roxie said with a wobble of her head. "I'd probably lose my mind trying to get used to being called Chloe again."

"It's fine. I just wanted to ask."

"Thanks for that." Roxie put her hand on June's shoulder and squeezed.

Dinner came and everybody focused on their individual dishes for a while. Roxie had a steak that melted in her mouth and would have asked for another, it tasted so good, but she was about to burst. All she had room left for was a piece of cake, and Kai brought that out with his staff in tow. There were sparklers and balloons around the large round cake decorated with whipped cream swirls and lemons.

"Is that?" Roxie started to ask Lincoln, but he nodded before she could finish.

"Your favorite lemon baked cheesecake from Mama's Bakery. The one back home." He smiled tentatively, as if worried it might not be her favorite anymore.

"My goodness, you are full of wonders today." She leaned over to kiss him in thanks and waited for the cake to be brought to her. She blew out the candles while she made her wish, for the love to never end, and then took the first piece when June had sliced the cake.

They were ordering coffee to go with the cake when Lincoln leaned over to tell her he'd left his phone in the car. "I won't be long."

"Okay. Hurry back." She leaned over to kiss him without a second thought and went back to talking to her friends.

"So, tell me what happened with you and Lincoln," June asked once Lincoln was gone.

"I don't know, really." Roxie tried to think of how to explain it all. "That night of the fire, well, he took me home and we saw the blaze. There were some men there that had been at the house before, do you remember that?"

"Yeah, I do. They were there that night? Those Italian-looking guys?" June asked, frowning.

"I guess they could have been Italians, yeah." Roxie nodded. "Well, he took me out of town, and well, something happened that night, but I left the next morning. I didn't want to involve any of you in that mess if those guys were after me too. I ran, came here, built up my life."

"Okay. I guess he found you finally?" June asked, but they both knew the answer to that.

"Yeah. I can't believe he was looking for me all that

time." Roxie sighed and leaned on her elbows, head in her hands, on the table. "I still can't believe it."

June looked at her in a weird way, making Roxie frown. "What?"

"Maybe I was wrong about him." June finally answered after another long speculative look at Roxie.

"What do you mean?" Roxie asked, wondering if her friend had the same suspicions she did.

"Maybe it wasn't that he was incapable of love. What if the only woman he's ever loved is you?" June continued to look at Roxie, her eyes searching. "Are you prepared for that?"

"I wasn't when he first came back into my life. I didn't want love at all. I still don't. But I care about him a lot more than I should. I'm opening up all these doors now, doors that should probably stay shut to keep you all safe, but he just makes me want to fling them all open, consequences be damned."

"Even if that means you get hurt in the end?" June asked, and Roxie realized that June was being protective of her brother. In an odd way, that pleased Roxie greatly.

Lincoln needed someone in his corner and June was a great person for that job.

"I promise, I'm not going to be the one that hurts him, June." She touched her friend's elbow. "I know what he's putting at risk, and I respect him too much to just throw that away like it doesn't matter. And listen, I know the reputation that women in my line of work have, but I'm not after him for his money."

"I didn't think you were. I just wasn't sure if you knew how fragile he really is. He's never had a long-term girlfriend that I know of, and it's clear what he feels for you. I can see it in his eyes when he looks at you."

"Do you see that same look in my eyes, June?" Roxie asked, knowing she did.

"I do. And I'm worried for you too. What if we're wrong?" June looked tortured, her lips pursed and her eyes stormy. "I'm happy for you both, if you're both happy, but I'm worried about you both. You're both such stubborn assholes sometimes."

Roxie laughed at that and hugged her friend close. "Oh, that hurts. I'm not nearly the asshole he is."

"You are too. Remember when I wouldn't buy a pink and purple tutu just because you wanted mine to match yours? You put pink and purple dye in my hair when I was asleep at your house." June reminded Roxie of the one time June had tried to go blonde, and Roxie had ruined it.

"Hey, that look is in now." Roxie grinned but sighed. "Sorry about that. Yeah, I was an asshole when I wanted to be."

"I forgave you a long time ago," June said, and gladly took the cup of coffee the waiter brought. "I'm so tired.

At least I have the next few days off. I put in for some vacation time."

"Oh, good. We can catch up properly then." Roxie's grin grew huge as she tried to think of everywhere she'd take her friend. "You can rest tomorrow and then I'll show you the best places to see here."

"I'd love nothing more than to sit on Lincoln's deck, watching the ocean, actually. Would that be okay for day one, at least?" June asked, and Roxie saw how tired she was when June let the mask slip a little.

"Whatever you want, babe. I'm not forcing you into anything." Roxie picked up her own coffee and traded seats with Trevon to talk to Emily. Emily had signaled to her so Roxie went to see what she wanted.

"Lincoln told us not to bring presents," Emily whispered. "But he told us this party was for you. Though he didn't tell us it was your birthday. I got you this."

"Emily, you didn't have to get me anything, you know that." Roxie protested but Emily forced a box into her hands.

"I did. You have given me so much, Roxie. I don't think I'd be where I am right now without you, and I don't think I ever thanked you properly for that. So whether it's your birthday or not, I saw this and got it for you. Take it, please."

Roxie looked down at the black and gold jeweler's box and opened it. A pair of gold angel wings formed a pendant attached to an 18k gold necklace. "It's beautiful."

Roxie breathed the words out as she pulled the necklace from the box by the pendant.

"I'm glad you like it. You've always been there for me, and really, you're my angel." Emily sniffled but blinked away the tears. "I will love you forever, whatever you may have had to do, or the secrets you've kept over the years. I love you, my friend."

"Aw, Emily. Don't make me cry." Roxie protested as she hugged her friend around the neck. "You deserve every bit of happiness you have now, no matter how you got it. I love you too, honey."

"I'm so glad." Emily pushed a lock of blonde hair behind her ear and smiled a watery smile at Roxie. "I want the full story as soon as you're ready to tell me."

"I will," Roxie assured her, looking around for Lincoln now. "Have you seen Lincoln come back in?"

"No, where did he go?" Emily asked, looking around too.

"He went to get his phone. He might have had to hunt down the parking attendant or something. No worries." Roxie smiled, but the air felt different around her. She felt stifled all of a sudden and worry gnawed at her belly.

Kai started to go back to his seat and Roxie caught his hand. "Kai?"

"What's up, Rox? Everything okay?" Kai asked, a patient smile on his face.

"Have you seen Lincoln? He went out a while ago to get his phone but he hasn't come back in that I know of."

"Ah, maybe he went to the bathroom. If he's not back in a few minutes I'll look for him, alright?" His smile was confident, but Roxie couldn't shake that weird feeling that something was wrong.

"Yeah, sure. Thanks." She replied but her eyes were glued to the front door, not the hallway where the bathrooms were. The more seconds that passed, the more fear took over. Something was wrong.

15

Roxie

"I'm going out to check on him," Roxie said to her friends gathered around the table. They were ready to leave, but they were still waiting for Lincoln.

Roxie's skin was covered in goosebumps that just wouldn't go away and all of her senses screamed that something was wrong. Kai hadn't taken her worry seriously at first, but even he had started to look worried.

"I'll go check the bathroom, Logan would you go with Roxie to check outside?" Kai asked as he stood up from the table, buttoning his suit jacket as though it were a habit, something he did without thinking.

"Sure, Kai. Keily, you want to come with us?" Logan asked, taking his wife's hand when she stood up.

Only it wasn't just Logan and Keily who came with her as she went out of the restaurant, it was all her friends but Kai. Even the head waiter came out with them. The man's name was Bill and he was busy berating the parking attendant, but Roxie wasn't sure why.

"Do you know where the car is parked?" Roxie asked the attendant when Bill took a breath in between dressings down.

"Yes, ma'am, I'll show you. I tried to tell Mr. Young I'd bring the car around for him, but he insisted he was fine. I'm sorry." The young man whose nametag read Jim spoke to her softly, his head down.

"It's not your fault, Jim. Please show me now." Roxie said, and they all began to walk towards the parking lot.

Roxie smiled briefly when she thought about how it must look to outsiders, all of the guests leaving at once like they were running out on paying the bill. Kai owned the place though, so that wouldn't be one of his worries.

It felt as if they'd walked for hours by the time they reached the car, and Roxie really regretted wearing the heels she had on instead of sandals, but the sight of the car coming into view made everything else fade into the background. The driver's side window was smashed in, and the door had been left open.

Roxie sped up to get to the car faster and saw that the keys to the car were on the ground. She picked them up without thinking, her eyes on the glass that covered the ground. Inside the car, she saw Lincoln's phone, but not Lincoln.

"Holy fuck." She mumbled, the blood rushing in her ears and fear strangling her throat until she couldn't breathe. She almost fell but somebody caught her in time.

"Steady on, Rox," Trevon said, and she absently put a hand over his where it was wrapped around her shoulders to hold her up. "I'm calling the police."

June came up beside her as Trevon placed the call, taking Roxie into her arms so that Trevon's hands were free. "He's been taken? By who?"

Obviously Lincoln hadn't filled June in on everything, Roxie thought, but she was too busy thinking of worst-case scenarios to fill in the blank spots. Tears streamed from her eyes unchecked. "It has to be Nathan."

"Your ex?" June probed, her eyes on the shattered window of Lincoln's car.

"Yeah, him." Roxie swiped at her face and tried to calm herself down. None of this would help Lincoln. "Trevon, are the police on their way?"

"Yep, should be here any minute now." He answered, his captivating eyes following Wendy as she came up to check on Roxie.

"What's going on?" Wendy asked, taking Roxie's right hand in hers. "Is he gone?"

"Yeah." Roxie looked back at the crowd standing behind Lincoln's car and noticed more people had joined her friends. Nosy people trying to figure out what was going on and if any of it was worthy of filming for their social media, no doubt, she thought with a hateful glare at the unfamiliar faces.

The police roared up a moment later with sirens blaring, but that didn't relieve Roxie at all. She could already see Detective Slater's perpetually hateful face in one of the cars and that almost drove Roxie over the edge. If that bitch sneered at her one time...

"Who's the sour-faced cow?" June whispered to Roxie, making her smile briefly.

At least she wasn't the only one that noticed the detective's sour demeanor. "A detective. I've dealt with her before."

"Ms. Simpson." The detective drawled as she strode up to Roxie, thumbs hooked in her gun belt. "Tell me why I'm not surprised you're involved in this matter?"

"Because you're a giant inflamed asshole of a bitch?" The words slipped out before Roxie could stop herself but once they were out, she decided she didn't give a fuck. The woman was exactly that and it was time somebody told her. Just in case she didn't already know.

The detective stared at her with lethal death-glare levels, but Roxie didn't back down. Instead, she raised her chin and stared down at the much shorter detective. The detective's glare cooled down when a policeman in uniform came up to her and placed his hand on her elbow.

"Detective Slater, you need to see this." The man with Anderson written on his badge said.

The woman walked away, her back ramrod straight.

"I can't believe you said that to her." Wendy snickered once the detective was out of reach, her gleeful smile on Roxie.

"She's had it coming. She's lucky I'm not the violent type, the way she's treated me." Roxie paused to frown. "But then, I'm probably the lucky one, the woman is a cop, after all."

"Well, she can't put you in jail for calling her out on her attitude," June said and looked around. "Why don't we go back inside the restaurant? We can all wait in there. I'm sure the detective will have questions."

"Oh, she will." Roxie nodded vigorously, but followed behind June without debate. "She always has questions."

"You're right." Wendy agreed, her hand coming up to take Roxie's elbow in support of her friend. "That woman is a piece of…"

"Hey, what's going on? I checked around the bathroom and the kitchen, everywhere I could think of that he might be, whether he had a reason to go there or not." Kai said as he came running up to them.

"I doubt you'll find him inside. Something has happened. The driver's side window of his car has been smashed in, his keys were on the ground, and his phone is still in the car." Roxie informed him, a little peeved that he hadn't taken her seriously to begin with.

With all the drama that was taking place in her life, he should have known better than to dismiss her worries. Sure, Lincoln could handle himself in most situations, and no, he hadn't been a target for any of the people that wished to harm Roxie, but things changed.

Roxie felt bad for her moment of anger, but she couldn't help the lingering resentment. Who knew where Lincoln was and the more time that passed, the further away he could be, or the more danger he could be in. Fuck, why hadn't Kai listened?

"Let's get some more coffee and wait for the detectives," June said, her grip on Roxie's other elbow a little tighter.

Roxie looked over at her long-lost friend and felt shame wash over her. Of course, June was his sister, she'd be just as upset, if not more so. "I'm sorry, June. I didn't even think about you being his sister."

"It's okay, Roxie. It's been a long time, and you're upset." June took her old seat and Roxie followed suit.

Wendy took the seat Lincoln had sat in while their other friends stood around, trying to figure out how to help.

"Do you want coffee or something harder? Maybe both?" The waiter that had served them all night asked.

"A shot of bourbon and a cup of coffee for me, please," Roxie answered, hoping the alcohol would steady her nerves.

"I've got my team out searching for him," Kai said as he came back in. Roxie noted how Kai sat on June's other side behaving almost as if he were her boyfriend but didn't say anything about it. Now wasn't the time to point out anything like that.

Roxie had downed the bourbon and was halfway through her coffee by the time the detective came in and zeroed in on Roxie. "Right, tell me what you know."

"I know what you know. He went out to get his phone and he didn't come back. We didn't think anything of it at first, but I started to wonder what was keeping him."

Kai took up where she left off. "When we grew concerned, I went to check the bathroom while Roxie and everybody else went to check outside."

"Hm, okay." The woman drawled as if she didn't believe a word either said. "And I suppose you're going to tell me this has something to do with that boyfriend of yours? Or did you break up with him before you moved on to the rich guy?"

Roxie's blue eyes turned to ice as she glared at the detective over the insinuation. "The man has assaulted me twice now. Do you really think I'd stay with him? And I didn't move on to the rich guy, as you put it. Lincoln and I are old friends."

"But you're sleeping with him, right? Maybe your old boyfriend isn't happy about that?" The detective pressed, her eyes just as hard as Roxie's.

"I'm going to let most of this slide, detective, since you're investigating why he's gone missing. But keep on and I'll report you for being unprofessional and whatever else I can think of." Roxie said evenly, her head high as she looked down her nose at the woman, even though Roxie was the one sitting down.

"Whatever. Do what you like. People like you, well..." The woman's voice trailed off as another detective came in. It would seem her poison tongue could be stilled, then.

Roxie was certain she didn't want the other detective hearing how she spoke to Roxie but didn't care. "Listen, I don't care what you think of me, just find Lincoln. Do your job for once, won't you? If you'd found Nathan sooner this might not have happened."

"Oh, so you know it was your ex? How do you know that?" Detective Slater asked, her eyes bright with triumph, as if she'd managed to catch Roxie in a lie.

"I don't, I'm just assuming it has something to do

with him. Lincoln may have other enemies, he's a businessman, it happens, but I doubt this is anybody but Nathan's doing." Roxie decided to shut up when the detective's eyes didn't change.

Roxie doubted she'd ever know what the woman's problem with her was, and didn't really care if she did, but she did want the woman to do her job. Saying anything that might implicate herself was stupid and maybe antagonizing the woman wasn't smart either. "Kai, can you tell her anything else?"

The detective's attention turned to the handsome Chinese man whose wealth surpassed anything Roxie could imagine. She noted the way the detective turned polite, almost subservient as she spoke to Kai. Roxie could barely hide the way she rolled her eyes, but the detective wasn't looking at her now, thank fuck.

An hour passed before the detective said they could all leave. Roxie was going to call a cab, but Dylan walked up and offered to take her home. Roxie gathered her things and left with Dylan and Emily. Emily sat in the backseat with Roxie while Dylan drove to Lincoln's house.

"Would you two like to come in for a few minutes? I could use the company." Roxie was extremely tired suddenly, despite the coffee, but didn't want to be alone just yet. She knew more people would stream in, June, Mandy and Tanya, maybe even Kai and

Trevon, but she would be alone until one of them arrived.

"Of course, Roxie, anything you need, babe. I told you that earlier." Emily hugged her close as Dylan turned the car off.

Roxie saw even more security personnel on the grounds of the house and while it made her feel safer, she couldn't help but wish they'd all been with Lincoln earlier. She nearly fell apart as they walked up the steps, but she got herself under control again.

"Can you tell me what exactly is going on?" Dylan asked once they were in the house and seated around the kitchen table, more coffee brewing on the counter. Roxie doubted she'd get much sleep, even if she tried.

"I don't know where to start," Roxie said, her lips pursed as she tried to figure out exactly what was going on. "I've known Lincoln all my life, really. When I was eighteen, my parents died in a fire."

"I'm so sorry about that, Roxie," Emily said, understanding dawning on her face. "That's why you hate electronics. I thought it was the fire at Elmo's."

"That made it worse, actually." Roxie conceded, before she filled them in on the men she'd seen the night of the fire, and how she didn't know if it was them, Nathan, or the people after Nathan that took Lincoln.

Roxie's head was in her hands as Dylan asked another question. "Do you think it was something to do with his business instead of to do with you? Maybe he pissed off a rival, or something like that. It might not be to do with you at all, Roxie."

"I guess anything is possible. I don't see Lincoln getting mixed up in any kind of deals that would result in this though. He's always organizing parties for charitable events, volunteering his time, and actually working to help those in need. I don't see him getting involved in anything shady and lately, he's always at home. People really love Lincoln, because he earns it. I can't think of anyone that would want to hurt him, not from his life, only mine." Her throat closed on the last word, and she couldn't hold back a sob.

Emily took her friend in her arms and tried to soothe her, but the dam had finally broken. Lincoln was gone and it was her fault, Roxie sobbed over and over again. She was still sobbing when June and Kai came in. June knelt beside Roxie to add her arms to Emily's encircling her.

"Roxie, you stop blaming yourself right now. My brother adores you unlike anything I've ever seen before. He would hate knowing you're blaming yourself. None of the blame lies with you, anyway. It rests with whoever was stupid enough to take him. And they better hope the police find them, whoever it is that took him, because if Kai finds them first, they'll wish they'd never set eyes on either of you."

Roxie wiped at her face, her eyes aching from her tears. "I hope he cuts their balls off."

"That'll be only the beginning, my love," June said, her eyes hard and almost as reassuring as Lincoln's were. "I promise you that Kai will make them pay, no matter what."

16

Lincoln

The night was going great, he thought as he walked out to the car, pausing to stare up at the sky. The streetlights made it almost impossible to see the stars, but he knew they were up there, looking down on him. It was one of the things he missed the most when he wasn't in Cambodia, how well he could see the stars.

His hands were in his pockets, and he felt good. Roxie had revealed one of her secrets to her friends, the biggest one as far as he was concerned. She probably had more secrets than that, but he wouldn't push her anymore. He had a big one he hadn't quite revealed yet either.

The time had never seemed right to talk to her about the way her parents died. Bringing up that night caused her pain, crushing pain that wrote itself all over her face whenever it was mentioned. He'd decided to wait until the time was right, for good reason, but if he didn't tell her soon, he might come to regret it.

The salty scent of the ocean wafted on a cool breeze, the summer smell conflicting with the sensation of winter. Lincoln knew that the people that lived on the coast year-round were probably used to that smell, but he still thought of summer when he smelled it. Smiling at his sudden poetic streak, he started to head for the car, realizing how much time he'd wasted already.

The attendant told him where the car was parked so he had no trouble finding it as he moved through the rows of neatly parked vehicles. He clicked the button in his pocket and reached for the door handle to open the car. He spotted his phone in the center console and frowned. How could he have forgotten it when it was right there?

Roxie's fine ass getting out of the car flitted through his mind, and the memory of how he'd wanted to get out of the car as quickly as possible to touch that part of her was all the explanation he needed. Yep, she distracted him to no end, but he didn't mind a bit.

Lincoln started to bend to reach for the phone when

a hand wrapped around his face and a cloth covered his mouth and nose. Whoever it was attacking him was shorter than he was and had to reach up to keep the cloth over his face. Lincoln reacted automatically, his elbow flying back, his fingers dragging the keys out of his pocket where they dropped on the ground, but he didn't notice. He was hoping to crack a rib, but his elbow caught the window instead, shattering the glass all over the ground.

Lincoln grabbed at the arm around his waist, tearing fingers back until the man screamed when they tore out of their joints, but he didn't let go of Lincoln's face. Lincoln felt the world going dark, tried to stay in the moment, in the present, but it was getting harder. His foot came down sluggishly on the man's foot, but it wasn't forceful enough and resulted only in a groan.

Lincoln's body wavered as the cloth cut off his air, forcing him to inhale even more of the fumes. He reached out one last time, going for the man's injured hand, causing him to let go at last, but Lincoln was out before he even hit the ground.

LINCOLN HEARD a roaring sound as he came back to the world but thought the pain in his head must be causing the noise. His thoughts spun around, trying to figure out where he was. Was he at home?

He tried to move, but his arms were tied behind his back and his feet seemed to be tied up too. He knew he wasn't at home. Roxie had no reason to tie him up like this and leave him. Sure, she'd tied him up in the playroom, but the rough wall that his face was pressed into wasn't like anything in the playroom.

Roxie.

The party.

Going out for his phone.

Memories played in his mind as he used the wall to pull himself up to a sitting position. That's when he figured out the roaring sound wasn't in his head, it was outside. He must be near the ocean, that was the sound he heard, the rush of waves as a storm came in. He could even smell the unmistakable smell of the sea now, too.

Where the fuck was he?

And who the fuck had gotten the best of him?

Lincoln moved around, trying to get his hands out of the rough rope tied around his wrists. The rope didn't budge at all, it only chafed his skin as he rubbed his wrists together, trying to force them out of the bonds.

The rope around his feet was a little looser, but try as he might, he couldn't free his feet either. Fuck, if the guy had used zip ties, he could have worked his way out of those. This might be harder.

Lincoln moved around on the floor, working until he felt as though his shoulders would pop out of their sockets, but he was finally able to roll around enough to get his hands in front of his body at least. Fuck, this was a mess, he decided as he took a break from his escape attempt.

He felt like an idiot for letting this happen. He should have made sure the security team followed them to the restaurant when they left the house. He should have made sure he had his phone. He should have sent someone else to get the phone. He certainly should have been able to take the guy that assaulted him. He didn't even want to think about what it must have looked like as he rolled around on the floor trying to get his hands under his ass and then his legs through too.

This was not only humiliating, it was also embarrassing. Kai would be on it, though. Lincoln had no doubt about that, at all. Roxie and June were probably about to lose their minds, but that couldn't be helped. Kai would know what to do to get him back, if Lincoln couldn't free himself, that was.

With numb fingers, Lincoln tried to work at the rope around his ankles. The rope around his wrists had only grown tighter through his struggles, not looser as he'd hoped. Still, he managed to free his ankles at last and sprang up from the concrete floor. He was a little dizzy for a moment, but the sensation passed.

The space he was in was completely dark. The dark seemed to eat any light, almost like a black hole. Well, what he read black holes were like, darker than dark, a void that made no sense, but was there, nonetheless. He started to walk with the wall against his right shoulder. It wasn't a huge room, but big enough. Probably a storage space, since there were no windows at all.

Lincoln had hoped there were windows and that they were just covered. Without a way out, he wouldn't be able to escape. He kept walking until he stumbled. The wall had changed. Holding his hands out in front of his body, he felt the structure and frowned. It was metal with grooves and then solid pieces jutting out from the grooves. Like a security shutter in a storage building.

Okay, he didn't know exactly where he was on a map, but he did know what he was in, a storage building. That was something anyway.

Weren't they notorious for having shitty locks? Lincoln felt along the bottom of the shutter but then realized it was pointless. The lock was outside, a padlock most likely.

"Fucking hell!" He shouted, anger fueling the sound of his voice. "Let me out of here, dickhead!"

There was no answer, just the sound of the rushing waves somewhere outside.

Looked like it was up to Kai to work this out then, he decided and went to sit down in a back corner. He didn't want to be up front in case the guy came at him with a weapon. He'd probably have one if he came back.

The good news was, Lincoln was still alive. Which meant whoever had taken him wanted him alive. This was probably about money, ransom. Nathan's face came to mind and Lincoln decided that if he ever got out of this, he would smash that prick's face in and end the man so that he'd never be a problem again, for him or Roxie.

He wasn't worried, the fact that he was still alive told him all he needed to know. Whoever it was either wanted information or money. Lincoln would stall for time if it was information, giving Kai time to find him. If it was money, he'd arrange it all himself, once the guy showed up to make the deal.

The asshole would show up eventually, Lincoln knew that much.

He looked down at his wrist, wanting to check the time, but his watch was gone. What a fucking petty thief, he thought, his rage only growing as he brooded there in the darkness. It had to be Nathan, anybody else would have left the watch.

His headache was easing, but his eyes were burning for sleep. He tried to stay awake, to keep his eyes open, because he didn't want the man to open that shutter without him knowing the guy was coming. When he found himself nodding off, he'd force himself up the wall and to his feet. Eventually, he grew too tired to get up again, and he waited there, trapped in the darkness.

Why hadn't Kai come already, he wondered, knowing hours must have passed. Maybe he was outside, waiting on whoever had dumped him here to show up. Yeah, that made sense, Lincoln decided. It would do no good to rescue him without knowing exactly who it was that took him in the first place. He wanted to know so he could beat the guy's face to a pulp. Good plan, Kai.

With his head back against the wall, Lincoln tried to keep himself awake. That became uncomfortable soon enough and he slid down on his back. He'd hear whoever was coming, these places usually had gravel outside, and he'd be able to get back up on his feet then.

Lincoln tried to think of things that would fuel his anger, keep him awake, but he'd been knocked out with some kind of drug, and it was late. Which only made him laugh, who knew chloroform was still a thing? He thought that shit was only used in old movies and books. Still, it was a good tactic for someone on their own facing off with a superior adversary they wanted to kidnap.

His thoughts were getting loopier, the longer he was locked up in that dark room. For some reason, a memory of his mother came to him, long before the other kids came along. She was in the living room, crying in the semi-darkness, sprawled out on the couch with a picture in her hands. Lincoln had been too small to know why his mommy was crying, but he was old enough to know she wouldn't want him to go to her. Even if the urge to make her stop crying was overwhelming him.

It must have been his dad, or maybe someone else, he decided as his eyes closed and his breathing evened out. He jerked awake when he realized he was dreaming.

"Got to stay awake." He said, but he noticed his speech was slurred. It had been a long day for him, one he'd expected to end in bed with Roxie. Being kidnapped hadn't been part of the plan at all and he needed sleep now.

"No time for sleep. Got to stay awake."

He tried to get up from the floor, but he was exhausted. He did manage to sit up, his back against the wall. Roxie, he told himself, think of Roxie. Her smile and laugh, the way she looked at him in utter delight when she saw the ring and the bangle he'd bought for her. He knew he should have given her her mother's watch back, but he'd forgotten all about that thing until now.

It was ugly to him, a gaudy display of wealth, but he could see why it had caught Roxie's eyes when she was a teenager. It was sparkly, shiny, and everything that he knew would catch a teenage girl's eyes. He'd put it in his safe and forgotten about it. He'd give it back to her when he got out of this mess, he decided. It was her mother's so he couldn't sell it off to replace the money he'd lost. Besides, Roxie was worth every penny.

His smile was crooked, but he couldn't see that in the dark. All he knew was that making her happy made him happy. And she'd be very unhappy if he didn't get out of this mess alive. He had another go at trying to free his hands and wondered if a trick he'd seen online would work. It took some fiddling around with fingers that were still kind of numb, but he eventually managed to tie his shoestrings the way he wanted and started to work his feet against the rope. Friction had worked in that video, but it had worked on a zip tie. The rope wasn't budging.

"Fuck!"

The shout echoed around the empty room, but he didn't care. Pissed off all over again, he redid his shoestrings properly and tried to think of a way to free himself. Nothing came to mind. And even if he got his hands free, what then? The lock was still on the outside of the building and as far as he knew, there was nothing in the room that he could use to force the door open.

Momentarily defeated, he leaned back against the wall and rested. When he felt himself snore softly, he forced his eyes open and leaned forward. Nope, no sleeping. Roxie needs you to go back home in one piece. Come on. Wake up.

He was about to force himself to stand up again when he heard the scrape of gravel beneath tires. A sound like a car engine soon reached his ears. He was about to find out who'd taken him. And who he was going to have to kill for daring to do it.

17

Lincoln

*H*e stood up as the car stopped outside. He heard the car door close and feet against the gravel. He prepared himself for a fight as the padlock was removed and the shutter came swinging up.

"Don't try anything or I'll shoot, then where will we be?" A voice called out of the darkness.

Lincoln agreed, it would do no good to try to sweep the man's legs out from under him, he'd just knock the guy down and have to scrabble back up to try to get the man's gun, if he even dropped it. He stood there, blinking as the car's headlights filled the space with bright piercing rays.

"Fuck, why did you leave the high-beams on?" Lincoln protested.

"Shut the fuck up." The man said as he walked into the small room and stared at Lincoln.

He was strung out, skinnier than he was not that long ago, with greasy hair and eyes huge in his now skeletal face. Lincoln's smirk intensified when he saw the man's left hand was wrapped in a beige bandage. He took pride in knowing the man's injury was his doing.

"Damn man, what are you on that's making you rot so fast?" Lincoln didn't back down, choosing to antagonize the man instead.

"Don't fucking worry about it, rich boy. Sit down and shut up." Nathan's ruined voice grated out from lips too big for his face now. There were blisters around his mouth and on his lips.

Meth or crack, Lincoln decided as he sat back down, following orders. Both would make Nathan unpredictable, cloud his thinking, and make him even more stupid than he already was. Great, just what he needed to deal with right now.

"I'm going to talk now and you're going to listen." Nathan insisted, waving the gun at Lincoln sideways like an idiot.

"You know if you shoot the gun that way that it's only going to jam, right?" Lincoln couldn't help saying it. Only morons would try to shoot a gun that way.

"What?" Nathan asked, his pitiful imitation of a tough guy momentarily wavering before he brought the gun up the right way. "Whatever, man. Listen, I'm going to prison for arson at the very least. Then there's the people that I probably shouldn't have stolen from."

"Including Roxie." Lincoln offered but Nathan didn't seem to appreciate his help.

"Shut the fuck up, I said," Nathan shouted, bouncing on the heels of his feet.

He could knock the guy over with a good shove, but he'd have to get to his feet first. Jumpy McJumpy Pants over there would probably shoot him from reflex if he tried that.

"I need ten million dollars, clean and untraceable. I'm getting out of this country and starting a new life somewhere else." Nathan said proudly, as if he was doing the world a favor.

"Actually, you'd probably only get through a few grand before you OD in some shitty motel and die. How about I give you 5k and we call it even?" Lincoln offered, his plan already in place.

"I'm going to get clean." Nathan insisted, swiping at his nose with his free hand. His nose was bleeding, and he didn't know it, but he smeared blood across his face when he did that. "I'm going to have the life rich boys like you take for granted. And I'm going to leave that bitch behind too. You can have her. I don't want her anymore."

"I'd be very careful if I were you, Nathan," Lincoln warned, his eyes deadly calm. The exhaustion was gone now, he wasn't tired at all, and he'd break the little shit's neck if he said another word about Roxie.

"Fuck her and fuck you too. I know shit, man, shit that would blow your balls off if you knew it." Nathan bounced again, making Lincoln wonder if he needed to pee.

"What shit, Nathan? I doubt you know anything at all, really."

"I do, man, I do. I found shit in her apartment, when I, uh, you know, broke in." Nathan's forehead wrinkled for a moment, but it smoothed out again as he grinned at Lincoln. "Give me my ten mil and I'll tell you every-thing I know."

"Hm. That's all? Why not ask for fifty million or a hundred? Why not a billion? Roxie doesn't have that kind of money and I can't do anything from in here with no phone."

"It's okay, I'm going to call her soon and tell her what she needs to know. I want ten million from you, *compadre*. She can ask her rich friends for the amount I'm going to tell her, don't you worry none." Nathan giggled as he revealed his plan to get double payments.

"And if you don't agree to pay me too, well, I'll take her money, shoot you, and still be fucking rich."

"Damn, I didn't know it was possible to be that fucking stupid," Lincoln replied, rolling his eyes. "I don't think anyone will be dumb enough to give you money without seeing me alive first. Or didn't you think about that part? You could just be cashing in on somebody else kidnapping me for all they'll know. They'll want to see me, and if I see anybody, I'll tell them your plan, dumbass."

"No, you won't, not if you want the info I've got. That's what your ten million is for. The information I've got. Hers will be to free you." Nathan nodded again, looking around as if he had an audience applauding him and he was acknowledging each new clap of hands.

He's high as a kite, Lincoln decided and sat back. This might take a while and he was tired. "Listen, let me go, and I promise, I won't kill you."

"Ha! Your hands are tied up, you ain't doing shit. Besides, I want to talk to Roxie first. Get my other ten million out of that whore before I do anything else. Fuck her and fuck you too." Nathan's brain seemed to go off somewhere for a moment and he stared up at the ceiling, the gun still pointed directly at Lincoln, but on his crotch now, not his head.

"Fuck, please don't squeeze that trigger by accident. I think I'd rather lose my life than my balls." Lincoln said, placing his tied hands over the general area as if to protect it.

"What? Fuck you, man. I'll be back." Nathan walked out, closed the shutter, and locked it before Lincoln could do anything.

That junkie was going to fuck around and find out what Lincoln could do with or without his fists, Lincoln thought, as he relaxed against the wall once more. Mention of information didn't phase Lincoln one bit, he knew who she really was, even if dickhead out there didn't. He'd string him along, however, promise him the moon if it meant he'd get out of here and back to Roxie, where he belonged.

The sun started to rise and the little room started to warm up, but not too much. Lincoln sprawled out on the floor and let sleep take him at last. It was obvious Kai had some kind of plan, otherwise he'd be out of here already, but if not, Lincoln had one of his own.

He woke up again around midday if the light coming through the crack at the bottom of the shutter meant anything. He needed to pee, and he hated to do it, but he had to go. In a moment of spite, he moved to the spot where Nathan would have to touch to open the shutter and relieved himself there. The thought pleased him and kept him going as the hours passed and nothing happened.

He had no idea what was going on out there, or if

anything was happening at all. He was hungry and thirsty, but he'd manage if this didn't take too much longer. He couldn't imagine why it would. Nathan would find a way to contact Roxie, she'd eventually relay that information to Kai, who'd be at her side if he knew what was good for him, and Kai would sort the rest.

Roxie certainly didn't have that kind of money, but Kai would be there to help. And if Kai wasn't there, and he'd better have a damned good reason if he wasn't, then June would be, and she'd figure out what to do. Lincoln didn't want Nathan getting away at all, he wanted to use the man as a punching bag before turning him over to the police, but he'd let him dream for a little while that he was rich.

For a moment, Lincoln almost felt sorry for the man. Almost. Lincoln was born into a rich family and he'd never known what it was like to go without. He'd never had to worry about paying bills or delaying medical attention because he couldn't afford to pay for the care. He'd never had to worry about how to buy food or tried to pass a check he knew would bounce until payday to get food. None of that had ever happened to him. But he had known what drugs and gambling could do.

Even private schools told them about drugs, and Lincoln had seen a friend or three go down that route. He'd avoided anything harder than alcohol for recreational purposes, especially since he was an athlete throughout his academic career. Later, he'd had too much to live for to get hooked on shit like meth or crack cocaine. Which might just be more of his pampered life showing, but he couldn't help the fact that his family was rich and didn't feel guilty about it.

If the man had gone to Roxie and asked for help a long time ago, none of this would have happened. She might have been able to help him before it got too bad. She wouldn't have been in Lincoln's bed now, but Nathan's life wouldn't have turned to shit.

He tried to remind himself that he shouldn't judge people, but Nathan had assaulted Roxie twice and now he'd kidnapped Lincoln. He wasn't feeling very charitable towards the guy. Besides, we all had to make tough choices, whether that choice was softened by a huge nest egg or not.

Fuck it, he thought and got up to pace again. The beam of light from the crack didn't illuminate much but Lincoln could see enough to know there was fuck all in the room that he could use to get out of here. He settled back down on the floor when he grew bored with pacing and thought about the ways he could make Nathan pay for this bullshit.

Time passed, he grew thirstier and hungrier, but nobody came for him. The more time that passed, the more he got pissed off. Okay, maybe doped up Nathan had forgotten about him, or passed out in his car somewhere, high off the profits from Lincoln's watch no doubt, but Kai should have come for him by now.

Surely, they hadn't all abandoned him.

Lincoln's thoughts turned dark as the sun started to set and he was still locked away in the storage building. What if nobody came for him?

Would he be found by whoever rented the building next? A shriveled-up corpse that nobody cared for.

That was just stupid, he told himself. Kai cared. June loved him. Roxie adored him. They must all be out there searching for him. Even if Nathan was slumped over dead in his own piss somewhere, somebody must be looking for him?

Roxie would have wondered why he'd disappeared, especially when he'd only gone out to get his phone, and someone would have gone out to look for him. Right? But what if they'd assumed he'd jetted off for some business deal or something? They'd try to call him, but his phone was still in the car.

Roxie might be so pissed off that she'd get somebody to take her home. But she knew him better than that didn't she? What if she didn't?

Common sense would prevail, though, right? She wouldn't assume he'd just run off and left without an explanation, she was too smart for that. But things had been rocky for them not long ago. Would that be enough to keep her from looking for him?

His family would assume, of course, that he'd vanished due to some business thing. He'd done it often enough before Roxie came back into his life, that they just might. But Kai knew there was danger. He'd know to look for Lincoln, wouldn't he?

The sunlight disappeared completely, and Lincoln's thoughts only grew worse. He was going to die in this shitty little empty building, and everyone would go on with their lives. Maybe it was the dehydration making him think like that, or hunger, or it could be shock even, but whatever it was, Lincoln had settled into a very dark place where he could imagine just what would happen if Nathan had overdosed and nobody came looking for him.

Maybe his PAs would notice his lack of communication, he thought with a bright spark of hope that died. No, they would assume he was just incommunicado again. He'd done that before too. But what about his business? People would start to notice he wasn't responding to calls or emails. How long would it take for someone to notice he was missing?

Too long, he was afraid.

If he managed to get out of this mess alive, he was going to have to change some things about his life. Not just for Roxie, but for himself and his family. He'd been alone so long, a peripheral on the edges of most of his family's life, that they might not notice he was gone at all before it was too late.

He'd need to build bridges back to them somehow. And make sure that Roxie knew he needed her in his life. That he wanted her in his life. A fancy ring and a bracelet on which he'd spent what amounted to pennies to him, didn't prove anything. Sure the thought behind each gift should show he cared, but would it?

Roxie was used to being treated badly, would she assume that he was doing the same thing? That he'd grown tired of her after her birthday party and moved on to someone else?

He couldn't picture it, couldn't see how it made any sense, but in the dark, alone, thoughts crept in that he couldn't get rid of. His tongue stuck to the roof of his mouth and that made everything worse. The human body could go without food for a long time, he knew that, but it needed water.

At least it wasn't hot outside anymore. Maybe he'd last a little longer since he wasn't sweating. Lincoln closed his eyes again, trying to call Roxie's smile to mind. He wanted to be with her again so much it hurt. Please, don't give up on me, he thought, just before sleep took him again. Please, look for me.

18

Roxie

"Why aren't you looking for him?" Roxie shouted at Kai as the sun set on another day. "What if whoever has him has killed him already?"

"Roxie, please." Kai soothed, his hands out flat before his body. "I know it doesn't look like I'm doing anything, but I am."

"What? What are you doing, Kai?" She cried, hating how helpless she felt as she stared out at the dark sky. "He's out there and he needs us."

"I know, Roxie. We need to be patient though. Let whoever has him contact us." Kai must have had a really strong grip on his temper, Roxie decided as she moved away from him to grab a bottle of water from the fridge.

They'd made her go to bed last night, but she'd got right back up an hour later. None of them had slept at all as the hours passed and nobody came forward with a ransom demand. The police hadn't called to relay any information, but Roxie didn't hold out much hope there. That snotty bitch wouldn't tell Roxie anything. On purpose.

"I'm sorry. I know you're doing your best." Roxie apologized and went outside to sit on the deck alone.

Logan and Keily had gone home, as had Dylan and Emily, but June was still there, as were Tanya and Mandy. Kitty and River sent messages through the hours, but they both had to work. Tanya and Mandy went about their normal tasks, holding down the fort for Lincoln.

Roxie paced until her legs started to cramp. She drank so much coffee her stomach started to burn. She went to the bathroom and cried in private. She let the others comfort her and tried to comfort June. She tried to sleep again but couldn't, so she got in her car and drove down to the gas station to buy cigarettes and a lighter.

The pack sat unopened on the table, the neon green lighter on top. She'd smoked, very briefly, during a very rough time in her life. She thought it would take the edge off, but when she found herself craving a cigarette one day, she quit. The pack sat there, just in case. She put her hand over the red and white box with black letters, as if drawing comfort from the poison inside. As if knowing it was there was enough.

It was a distraction technique, she knew. As a dancer, she'd never been able to cut herself to seek relief. She showed too much of her body for that. It was also because she was a dancer, and a damned good one, that she also never turned to drugs. Well, that and they took money she didn't want to waste. Every now and then she'd drown her worries in alcohol, but yeah, hangovers sucked ass.

Using the poison in the cigarettes as a distraction was all she could manage at the moment. She wasn't hurting herself, but knowing she could, even if it was just a single cigarette, somehow…helped. Not the smartest idea in the world, but she was going out of her mind with worry.

No matter what anyone said, she knew in her gut that Lincoln's disappearance was her fault. This had something to do with her and if she'd just stayed out of his life, he wouldn't be in this mess. If he was still alive.

That made her stomach cramp and her chest squeeze so tight she thought she'd be ill from it. She stretched her arms back, trying to ease the tension, but nothing really helped.

When she checked her phone for the millionth time,

saw the battery was fine and there were no messages, she put it back down. The damn thing wouldn't ring in her hand now, would it?

She got up, paced the deck some more, and waited. The waiting wouldn't be so bad if it didn't feel like she was holding her breath, even when she inhaled.

"You okay out here?" June asked as she came outside.

"No, not really. I'm losing my mind."

"Me too and I haven't even called my family yet. Mom and Liam will be so pissed if I don't call them soon. And my dad too. He still loves Lincoln like he's his own." June sat down, looked at the cigarettes on the table, looked at Roxie, then back at the pack. "Can I have one?"

"Um, you're a doctor, June. No." Roxie came to sit down with her friend. "I shouldn't have bought them."

"Doctor or not, my nerves are shot to shit. Do you know how many doctors lecture their patients about smoking and then light up as soon as they get off of hospital grounds? Too damn many. Give me one." June reached for the pack, but Roxie jerked it away.

"No. Get your own. I'm not contributing to your future bad health." Roxie slid the pack into her back pocket and glared at her friend.

"See, still a stubborn asshole." June glared but that soon melted into a pout. "I just want one."

"No!" Roxie said more forcefully. "I'm serious, if you want one go get your own."

"Fine. I'll be back in a little bit. Do you want anything?"

"No, just Lincoln home."

"Oh, honey, I know. I do too." June hugged her before she left.

Roxie felt bad about planting the idea in her friend's brain, but that didn't stop her from reaching for her phone again.

Still nothing.

She went inside long enough to grab her pink hoodie and walked back out to the deck. The phone was ringing, and she ran for it, jerking it up off the table.

"Hello?" She said into the phone, her hands shaking.

"Ah, Roxie. My favorite whore." Nathan's obnoxious words filtered into her ear and Roxie shuddered.

"Fuck you, Nathan, what do you want?" She looked around as if expecting him to pop up out of the darkness.

"Ten million dollars, baby. Ten million or the rich boy you've been whoring for is dead." He gloated, but the high-pitched girlish giggle that accompanied his threat blunted the desired result.

"You have Lincoln?" Roxie asked, suddenly calm now that she knew who had him.

Nathan having him was a million times better than the gangsters she'd run from for over ten years. Who knew what those assholes were capable of? Nathan was so strung out he probably didn't even have Lincoln tied up.

"I do, Princess Whores-a-lot." He giggled again.

"Could you be any more childish, Nathan?"

"Well, I can shoot your new boyfriend, if that helps?" He offered, drying up her fountain of sarcasm instantly.

"No, don't do that. What do you want me to do? I don't have ten million dollars." She was stalling for time as it finally occurred to her that Kai should be in on this phone call.

She ran into the house to find him and put Nathan on speakerphone when she found Kai in the living room. She gesticulated at Kai and he sat up, paying attention as Nathan began to speak.

"I want you to meet me with the money down at the marina. I'll give you a few hours, I know it'll take a little while to get that kind of money together. Of course, you know you can't call the police or anyone else right? Bring the cash and you can have your boyfriend back."

The line went quiet for a long moment, but then Roxie could hear him faintly giggling again. Fucking high, he was fucking high! She bit down on her lip to keep from shouting at him.

"Oh, and Roxie?" He added, as if he'd just remembered he was on the phone with her. "If I don't have the money by tomorrow at noon, I'm going to start cutting off parts of your man. Starting with the one part you're most familiar with in your line of work."

"Don't do that, Nathan. Don't hurt him." Roxie said it more for his own good than hers. Lincoln would kill him a million different ways if he did that. And he'd get the better of Nathan eventually, Roxie had no doubt of that. Nathan was too high to be any threat.

"I'll do what I please, whore. I'm the one in charge now. Not you and not that rich boy you've been fucking. Bye bitch." He hung up then, before Roxie could say anything else.

"Right. Let's take that in." Kai said, sitting back on the couch. "He wants you to meet him at a marina, but he didn't say which one."

"Yeah, I noticed that too," Roxie said, sitting down. "He's high."

"I kind of noticed," Kai responded bluntly but without judgment.

"Maybe he'll call back?" Roxie could only hope he would.

"We'll have to wait and see," Kai said, his eyes on his phone as he typed into it.

"I'm going back outside."

"Cool," Kai called out, making Roxie frown.

Kai was so weird sometimes.

Should she call the police, she wondered as she stared at her phone. Kai had told her this morning not to do that. His team would handle it. As far as Roxie could tell, they weren't doing much of anything. Frustration sent her back to pacing.

This really, really sucked. She knew who had Lincoln now, which was kind of a relief, but she felt as if she'd had a carrot dangled in front of her, only to have it pulled away. Lincoln wasn't far away, but where would Nathan have taken him?

She went back into the house and pulled out a laptop that sat around for anybody to use. She pulled up a map of the area and started scrolling around it. She couldn't figure out which marina Nathan might be talking about. They'd never gone to one together, and he'd never talked about one. She looked through a list of marinas nearby, but none rang a bell in connection with Nathan.

"Where would he keep Lincoln?" Roxie asked Kai when he came near on his way through the kitchen.

"Somewhere where there's no people, probably with no windows, or, if he's always that high, it could be anywhere. He might have him staked out on the beach for all we know." Kai shrugged, but then spoke again. "What we need is proof of life. And I'm not talking about a severed finger or any of that garbage. We need to see him and hear what's going on around him. Maybe we could figure it out from that."

"Okay. If he calls back, which he'll have to since I have no idea which marina he meant and it was a private number that he called from so I can't call back, I'll ask to see Lincoln."

"No, not see him, be specific. I'm not letting you anywhere near that douchebag. Lincoln will kill me when he gets home if I do." Kai shook his head with a frown on his face.

"Then how am I supposed to take him the money?" She asked, her own frown in place.

"I'm hoping it won't come to that. If it does, we'll think of something. Ask him to video call you." Kai said, offering something at least.

"Fine. But this better work, Kai or so help me, you won't have to worry about what Lincoln's going to do to you because I'll have already done it." Roxie glared up at him with fire in her eyes. She meant it, too. If this all failed and something happened to Lincoln, it was Kai she was coming for. Right after she took care of Nathan.

It might be irrational to blame Kai for all of this, especially when Nathan was taking credit for it, but deep down, she kind of blamed Kai too. He was the security guru that let his friend be snatched away right under his nose. And he was the security expert that still had no clue where Lincoln was.

Fuck, everything was frustrating her and now she was even more exhausted. Sleep would not come though, she knew that. The hours passed, nothing happened, and Roxie started to lose hope. Kai wasn't doing anything but playing some poker game and checking his phone every now and then.

June was chain-smoking outside, and Tanya and Mandy were upstairs with their girls. Roxie was alone again.

Wendy came over late, with the apology that she'd had to work at Lemon Fresh that night because her parents had some important meeting to go to. Wendy rolled her eyes at that part. She reached for Roxie and Roxie hugged the smaller woman back.

"Thanks for coming over," Roxie said and looked at the bag in Wendy's hand. "Snacks?"

"Snacks and one of those subs I know you like." Wendy took Roxie's hand and Roxie took her outside on the deck. "What's going on?"

"No news since Nathan called earlier. He's probably passed out somewhere or trying to get more drugs."

"He really asked for ten million?" Wendy asked, chewing at some of the gummy worms she'd brought with her.

"Yeah, like I have that kind of cash." Roxie rolled her eyes and shook her head. "I'm not made of money."

"No, but some of the people you know are." Wendy

reminded her. "Even Lincoln probably has that stashed in his mattress."

"That's rude, Wendy. But yeah, you're probably right. I'll check later." Roxie smiled despite herself, knowing there'd be no money there. "Thanks for coming over. I needed a laugh."

"That's what I'm here for. To take care of you." Wendy pushed over a pack of sour peach gummy candy and Roxie took it.

"You always did know how to do that better than anyone else." Roxie smiled over at her sweet friend with sad eyes. "Lincoln does a good job, but you bring me candy."

"I do. Who loves you, baby?" Wendy asked with a wink as she gobbled another gummy worm.

"You do, duh." Roxie chewed at another piece of candy and looked out at the darkness. "What am I going to do?"

"Well, if these men can't handle the situation by the time the sun sets tomorrow, we will, my friend," Wendy promised with a look in her eyes that made Roxie pause.

"How so?" Roxie asked, wondering exactly what Wendy meant.

"I don't know yet, but we'll think of something." Wendy hedged, looking away from Roxie.

There it was again, a side of Wendy that clashed with the image of the woman that Roxie knew. There was a lot more to this woman than she let on, but Roxie wouldn't push her for answers. It wouldn't do any good, even if she did, she suspected. Wendy was a closed book in a lot of ways. Roxie was too, and if she demanded to know all Wendy's secrets, she might just demand to know all of Roxie's in return. And that just wouldn't do.

19

Lincoln

Lincoln was hungry. Cold and then hot. And fuck, if his mouth wasn't a desert full of sticky cotton. He was certain he'd lost some skin on his tongue because it kept sticking to his cheeks or the roof of his mouth. He had a fever, but he wasn't sure why. Stress, perhaps. Could thirst cause a fever?

There'd never been a need for him to find out if it could. He'd been in actual deserts before with more water than could be found in this shitty little room of nothing. If he weren't so weak, he'd get up and pace, but he was drooping from hunger and dehydration. It was best to save his energy for when Nathan came back. Not that he needed much energy for a battle of wits against that asshole.

What had Roxie ever seen in him, he had to wonder, his knees pulled up so he could rest his wrists on them. A shower would be a beautiful thing right now, but that wasn't the biggest worry he had.

He wasn't even overly worried about dehydration. He was worried about Roxie and what she might be about to do. She was either trying to mount a rescue or extremely pissed off that he'd vanished on her. Either one was a definite possibility. He hoped she was doing neither.

Nathan was unstable and would do anything to get what he wanted, which made him a different kind of dangerous. Brute force, revenge, hate, these were things Lincoln could deal with. A man out of his mind on drugs, terrified of the fate he'd brought down on himself, willing to do anything to escape that fate but too high to keep his thoughts straight was a whole new level of hell Lincoln had no clue how to deal with.

The car came back, the shutter opened, and Nathan walked in with his bandaged hand wrapped around a plastic bag. Lincoln's mouth hoped it was water.

"Stay there," Nathan said, pointing a gun at Lincoln. "Don't move."

Lincoln watched him, noting how the bags under Nathan's eyes were bigger, his mouth drawn down in a frown that was more inability to control his facial muscles than anything. The hand holding the gun shook so badly Lincoln had to look away.

Nathan was either in need of more drugs or about to fall over. Lincoln watched, pondering how awful it must be to need a drug so badly you'd kill yourself for it. Pity made Lincoln calm, but anger diluted the pity. Yeah, okay, the guy was beyond help but that didn't mean he had to hurt other people. That's where the pity stopped, when the man's addiction intruded into the lives of others in a damaging way.

"You can have this once I leave." Nathan croaked after a long moment of staring at Lincoln, as if trying to figure out why the man was in the room. "I'm waiting to hear from Roxie. Once I do, I'll bring a phone and you can arrange to get me the rest of the money you owe me."

Lincoln didn't point out that he didn't owe Nathan a damn thing, he just kept his mouth shut. He needed the drink that was making the bag in Nathan's arm wet. It must be cold to do that, and Lincoln was certain that if he had the extra moisture in his body his mouth would be watering.

Lincoln nodded agreement when Nathan's right eyebrow perked up over his eye. "Yeah, I'll get you whatever you want, Nathan."

"Cool." Nathan mouthed but he didn't actually speak.

"You know it's going to take a while to get that kind

of money together, right?" Lincoln couldn't remember if they'd had this discussion already. His brain was fuzzy from the physical stress he was under. Or it could be that even his brain was drying up.

"Yeah, man, I know." Nathan shrugged and looked away, uninterested.

"Why are you doing this to me? I haven't done anything to you." Lincoln prodded, trying to get some kind of information out of the man.

Later, once he'd had some water, he'd think about wringing the man's neck out like a washcloth. He needed water first.

"You took Roxie from me, first of all," Nathan answered, anger flaring briefly to life in his eyes.

Lincoln would have reminded him that he'd left Roxie long before Lincoln came to town, but he knew that would go over the man's head. He'd have pointed out that he also destroyed Roxie's apartment and assaulted her twice but didn't. What was the point? There would be no logical answers from Nathan, everything would be twisted, even the things Nathan had done.

"Fuck it, I'm out. You can have this shit once I'm gone. Don't waste it." Nathan put the bag down carefully, keeping the gun on Lincoln, even though his hand still shook like crazy.

Nathan backed up out of the room, his eyes still on

Lincoln. Once the shutter was down and Lincoln heard the rattle of the padlock being closed, he moved to grab the bag. Two bottles of water, a plain hotdog men a bun, and a few candy bars. It was something anyway.

Lincoln drank half of the first 64oz bottle before he dug the hotdog out and ate it. A sigh broke from his lips, even if the hotdog was cold. His belly had food in it and water was making its way into his system. He'd be able to think better now, and maybe deal with this punk when he visited next.

Hours passed and Lincoln figured out he'd lost track of time. He didn't know if the sun had gone down or if it was about to come up. In the end, it didn't matter really. Had it been two days or three that he'd been locked up like this?

Another guzzle of water finished the first bottle, but there was one more. That one would have to last. For now, sleep was on his mind. The air in the room was colder but he didn't put his jacket back on. That was his pillow. Rolling down his sleeves, Lincoln lay back down and closed his eyes.

If he got out of this, he'd take Roxie back to Cambodia. They were happiest there of anywhere they'd been together so far. He'd give up his business or put it in the hands of someone that could run it for him, and he'd devote his life to making her smile every single day.

Kai would find out eventually who the men were

that took her parents from her and would have the problem dealt with. And if Roxie was in Cambodia with him, there'd be no reason to worry anymore. She'd be free of all of her worries and would be able to spend her days as she pleased.

He knew she'd miss dancing, but maybe she could teach ballet if he built her a studio there. He doubted many of the women in the village would want to learn exotic dancing, but then again, women from all walks of life had joined her classes. She'd have whatever she wanted, and she could do whatever she wanted just as long as she was safe.

His eyes opened for a moment but closed again. There'd been a noise outside, another car passing by. It wasn't Nathan because the car kept going past his prison.

Lincoln struggled up to his feet, surprised that he felt steadier than he had in a while. The shutter was cold against his hands as he pounded on the metal barrier, but he didn't notice. Adding a shout to the banging of his hands, Lincoln hoped this would work. It would put a dent in his plans, but he needed to get out of here.

After making as much noise as possible, Lincoln paused, waiting to see if anyone had heard him. There were no sounds from outside, nobody came to find out what all the noise was. Probably people that thought it was better to mind their own business or they were so far they couldn't hear his pleas for help.

Fuck.

Discouraged but not defeated, he went back to his space in the left corner of the room and sat back down. He'd find a way to get out of this mess, one way or another. The full second bottle of water beckoned to him, but he ignored it. He didn't need more water right now. He needed to save that in case he was here longer.

Briefly, anger flared to life. Why hadn't Kai retrieved him yet? He should have been able to track Lincoln down by now. Or were they still thinking Lincoln had just wandered off?

Something Nathan said gave him hope. He was waiting for Roxie to call him back. That meant Nathan had contacted her and made his ransom demand. So, if they hadn't known that something was wrong before they did now. That was good, Kai would be looking for him now, if he hadn't been before.

Lincoln wanted nothing more than to curl up in his bed with Roxie in his arms but knew it would have to wait for a while longer. Memories of falling asleep with her in his arms brought a smile to his face. She always smelled good, even when they were in the jungle. And her body fit into his perfectly.

He had never told her but that was one of his favorite things to do, spoon with her, whether it was on the couch watching a movie or in bed falling asleep. His world felt complete when she was in his arms. Sex with her was glorious, sure, but just falling asleep with her and waking up to her? That was awesome.

His brain replayed moments with her. The way she smiled at him shyly when she woke up to find him watching her. She'd scrub at her eyes and wipe her face, but then she'd reach out, cup his jaw with her hand, and everything would be absolutely perfect.

Roxie had been in his mind for a very long time. She'd always been there with his sister June in some part of his life, even if she was called Chloe in the earlier part. That's how he'd come to think of it all since the night her parents died.

The first part of his life, before he'd held her in his arms and touched her in more intimate ways than he'd ever thought would happen. She'd been so young then, and so had he. Childhood teasing had turned into a burning need to comfort her. That's when the second part of his life began, post-Chloe, post the world kind of making sense. After that night everything had changed for him. Especially when he came back to the hotel and found her gone.

Then his life had become a search for the woman that he couldn't forget. Every day of his life since then had brought some memory of her. The way she'd laugh and dance with June, the way she'd stared at Liam with adoration, but never at him. When she saw him, her eyes would change and the childish hate would replace the adoration. But that night her eyes had gleamed with wonder in the darkness, with soul-destroying despair, and back to wonder when he touched her with all the teenage infatuation he felt.

Now he had to wonder if the need to find her, the craving to feel her touch again, was just childish infatuation after all. Yeah, it might be, but he didn't feel like what he felt now was simple infatuation. He could walk away from infatuations. He couldn't walk away from Roxie.

In fact, he wanted more time with her, every second she had to give him. This wasn't mere infatuation then. There was no need to question his thoughts on that, he was actually happy he could feel something for someone who wasn't a part of his inner circle. Well, okay, she was a part, a major part, of his inner circle now but that was what was really amazing.

When he'd first found her, his only thought had been to protect her. He wanted her, she was even more desirable now, and damn if she wasn't good in bed, but she was more confident now, unafraid of pain or being hurt. She was brave, kind, and so much more than the Chloe who'd walked out of his life all those years ago.

She might have been all of those things back then,

she must have been to survive as she had, but now she wasn't afraid to be those things.

"She's perfect, really." He said out loud, to the darkness, to nobody.

His head started to throb and he picked up the full bottle of water and held it against his head. At least the fever was gone now, as was the dangerously dry mouth. He listened to the sounds of the night, the surf somewhere outside, the distant sounds of cars speeding by on a road, the cry of a bird that might have had its sleep disturbed. Life went on out there, completely unaware that he was trapped in here, panicking about how much longer he'd be locked away.

Roxie knew Nathan had him, would she be in tears or pacing the floor? A smile stretched his lips because he knew the answer to that. She'd be pacing the floor, glaring at Kai and telling him to do his job. She wasn't the kind to sit still and do nothing while she let other people deal with her problems. If he knew her, and he was certain he did, she would be going to every bank she could find to get money from. Or she'd have all of her friends doing that while she tried to figure out how to find him.

Poor Kai probably had no idea how to handle the furious tornado that was his Roxie. Lincoln himself wasn't always certain of how to do that and he knew her well. The poor guy was probably pulling his hair out by now, especially with June there adding to the fray. Those two women together, combined with his PAs and the other women that Lincoln knew would be there for Roxie, would make an army that real soldiers should think twice about discounting.

With a final smile, Lincoln's brain drifted into sleep, while he hoped that he'd soon be out of this place and back in the arms of the woman he was almost certain he loved.

20

Roxie

"Alright, this is what we know so far," Roxie said to the gathering of women in Lincoln's kitchen. She pointed out different things that she'd taped to the wall. One had a list of marinas, on another sheet of paper she'd printed out listed places they could get money from.

Her friends were gathered around the table in the late evening, even her new friend Keily was there with Emily, Kitty, and River. Tanya and Mandy were there too, both studying the pages taped to the wall.

"It's going to be hard to get that much money together, Roxie, even from the hotel," Emily spoke up, studying the list of places to get money. "We mainly deal in credit card transactions, we rarely see cash."

"And the banks are going to start asking questions if we go in and ask for loads of cash." Kitty pointed out. "I think there's a limit on how much we can withdraw from the ATMs, too."

"I've thought about all of that. I don't know how we might get it though." Roxie looked at Emily, the one out of all of them that grew up in a wealthy family and had dealt with cash flow.

Okay, Roxie grew up in a wealthy family, but she'd had a credit card, rarely cash. She had no idea how rich people gained access to large sums of money when they needed it. Emily would know, wouldn't she?

"We can do it, I know we can." Keily piped in. "Logan's already working on that for you. It'll just take time we may not have."

"I'm amazed by all of you, really." Roxie looked around at the faces she'd come to love, feeling that love grow as each contributed in some way to helping her get Lincoln back. Kai was in one of the rooms upstairs, doing fuck knows what. Not looking for Lincoln, not that she could tell. Which was why she'd called all her friends over to come up with their own plan.

"Alright, that brings me to our next problem. My dumbass ex told me to meet him at the marina with the money. He didn't say which of these dozens of marinas he meant." Roxie pointed at the page with the list and then looked back at her friends. "How can I figure out which one it is, or trace his number so I can call him back?"

"Marinas are fairly secure places." River said, her eyes on the list. "Boat people are protective of their boats and those of the people around them. I've been to a few parties at marinas, if you aren't supposed to be there someone will know."

"Okay, so we're looking for a place that isn't so big on security then. Do you know which of these it could be?" Roxie asked and River got up, as did Kitty.

It was Emily that had a possible answer though, surprising them all. "Jetty's is the worst. I know that because I had to dock one of my dad's boats there when it came loose during a hurricane. It was the nearest and, believe me, most lax marina I've ever seen."

"You docked a boat during a hurricane?" Roxie asked, impressed.

"Yeah, all of my brothers were in Europe and Dad was who knows where. I was left to take care of it." Emily shrugged as if it was no big deal. "I love boats, so it was a challenge for me. And as it turns out, could be an answer to the problem."

Roxie circled the name of the marina with a red pen and stepped back. "Okay, any others?"

"White's is pretty shitty too." River pointed at one at the bottom of the list. "I have a friend whose boat was lost because the dock collapsed one day out of the blue.

The lines snapped after a while and the boat just floated off without anyone contacting him for a week."

"That's terrible." Roxie sighed but traced a red circle around that one too. "Any others?"

"Not that I can think of." River answered and looked at the other women.

"I'm new here so I have no idea," Keily said with a sad look. "Sorry."

"I hate boats," Mandy said with a shudder.

"I'm new here too," Tanya answered, staring at the other page on the wall. "What's that Roxie?"

"It's a list of places I think Nathan might have Lincoln in. He's cracked out of his mind, but I'm guessing he realizes he has to keep Lincoln somewhere quiet, out of the way, with no way to escape. I could be wrong, he might be so far gone he's got Lincoln in a hotel somewhere, but I've narrowed it down to storage facilities and empty buildings. That made making a list hard because I don't know all of the empty buildings in the area. I don't know if he has a car either. I've assumed he must so that he can transport Lincoln, at least. So, let's say he borrowed a car, he'll keep Lincoln near him, so he doesn't have to walk far because he'll have to give the car back at some point."

"You've looked for storage facilities near marinas, right?" Kitty asked and Roxie nodded.

"Yep, I have. This one is near White's, I know." Roxie

pointed at one of the places she'd listed. "And this one is near Murphy's, but that place has a lot of security. I've been there."

"So, we think that might be where Lincoln is then? That storage place?" Keily asked, her eyes narrowed as she picked up her phone. "Should I call Logan and let him know to go over there?"

It occurred to Roxie then that none of the women had mentioned the police or using the security outside to get Lincoln back. She gave a brief rueful smile before she shook her head to Keily's question. "Not yet. I'm going to drag Kai out of his room at some point and make him pay attention, if I have to tie him to a chair."

"I don't think Nathan will hurt Lincoln, no matter what he might have said. He wants money, hurting Lincoln would be pointless. We can work with that, even if it means doing nothing more than stalling him." Emily spoke up, as if she'd been chewing over the thoughts. "If Kai really isn't doing anything, which I doubt, he's probably just trying to keep you out of the way, then we can fix this, Roxie. Don't you worry."

"I know we can, and I'm so grateful to all of you." Roxie smiled but Tanya caught her eye. "What's up?"

"I think we should tell Kai what we've figured out. I'm with Emily, he's trying to protect you by leaving you out of the loop. Lincoln is very, *very* protective of you.

He'd kill Kai if he let you get hurt or into trouble that you can't get out of."

"I see." Roxie sighed, wondering if she'd been wrong about Kai this whole time.

"He's a good guy," Wendy said as she walked in, late because she'd been doing the night shift at Lemon Fresh. "But if our girl wants her man back, we'll get him back."

Roxie smiled at Wendy and gave her a wave. "Thanks, babe."

"Anything for you, my love." Wendy blew her a kiss and sat down. "So where are we?"

"We think we've figured out where Lincoln is, and which marina dumbass wants me to bring the money to. That much cash is going to take up a lot of room so he'll either need a big car or a large boat to transport it in. I don't know of any boats he might own but I have to admit, the man had me snowed. I didn't know about the drugs or the gambling for far too long."

"Don't blame yourself," Wendy said automatically, knowing Roxie too well, and Emily nodded in agreement.

"None of us saw it, Rox. Like Wendy said, don't blame yourself." Emily sipped at the coffee in a white mug and sat back. "What else should we be thinking about?"

"I don't know," Roxie said and came back to the table and sat down. "How to get into the storage facility to check? Do we go in a pack and just start banging on buildings, or do I go in alone?"

"Not alone." The other women all said in chorus. Roxie smiled at that. They knew her well. She'd go off by herself if she had to in order to get Lincoln back. "That might not be the best idea, no, but if it comes down to it you know I will."

"That's not going to happen," Tanya said, her face full of fierce determination. "I'll stay on you every hour of the day if I have to. Lincoln will kill us too if something happens to you."

Tanya looked over at Mandy who nodded. They were both on dialysis but despite that, Roxie knew both women were tough as nails and would put her in her place if they had to. Plus, she didn't want Lincoln to kill either of them. Kai maybe, but not these two.

"Fine, I'll behave." Roxie agreed with a pout that soon melted away. "So, what do we do next?"

"I'll take one of the security guys outside with me to that storage facility." Tanya offered, getting up to type the name of the place in her phone. "I'll check it out."

"How are you going to get in at this time of night?" Roxie asked but Tanya just winked with a knowing smile on her pretty face.

"I have my ways, Rox, don't worry."

"Okay. I'll wait to hear from Nathan then, I guess." Roxie glanced at her phone but didn't pick it up. She'd cradled that thing for hours without it ringing again. She'd smash it with a hammer if she didn't need it when, and if, Nathan did call back.

"I'll get on to Logan and find out what he can do," Keily said and stood up to grab her bag. "I'll go by the hotel and text you when I know something."

"Alright. Yeah, if he can arrange the money for us, that would be better than trying to get it out any other way." Roxie looked around, at a loss. There was nothing else she could do but wait.

"I'll stay with you. Dylan can hold down the fort at the house." Emily got up and looked at Roxie. "I'll order us some food. Who wants what?"

It was late but everybody seemed to agree that tacos were in order, so Emily arranged that. Roxie walked outside to the back deck. The women inside were all talking about what they could do next, but Roxie needed a moment to herself.

She knew the women she'd managed to draw into her life were awesome, but she hadn't known they'd be this awesome. It was amazing to her that she was this lucky and knew she couldn't take it for granted, no matter what happened in the years to come. They were all special in their own ways and, for some reason, that made her want to cry.

She knew she could blame it on the current circumstances and being overwhelmed by the love they were showing her, but was it more than that? Was it really that hard to admit to herself that people loved her?

It had been hard to let people into her life after her parents died, but she'd come to trust Emily, Kitty, and River. Wendy had worked her magic on Roxie too, and she'd become another sister in Roxie's army of wonderful women. She loved them all, but for some reason, admitting to herself that they loved her was hard.

She'd been alone for a long time after that night and Nathan was the first man she'd really thought she loved. He'd thrown that love back in her face and even now, he was trampling all over the love she used to have for him. Lincoln had come along though, picking up the pieces that Nathan had left her in.

Losing him would shatter her completely. Sitting down and waiting wasn't her style, especially when doing that might lead to her being alone in the world again. Well, not totally alone, she thought as she looked back into the kitchen to see the women all working together to help her. But without him, the world would be a much darker place.

That's why she was trying so hard to get him back. She'd do whatever it took to make sure he was safe and back with her. Her phone buzzed and she looked down at it eagerly.

It wasn't a text from Nathan, it was a reminder that

she had a meeting in two days. One that she normally wouldn't miss for anything. Damn, she'd have to cancel it, she decided and picked up the phone to make a call.

Roxie waited as the phone rang. A woman's voice answered, elderly but still strong. "Roxie? What's going on? You don't normally call this late."

"Nothing, I just have to cancel our appointment. I won't be able to make it because I have something very important I'm dealing with here and I don't know when it will be sorted out."

"That's fine, we can arrange it for another time, you know that. I hope it's not something too worrying?" The woman asked with concern.

"It's being dealt with, but there's a lot that's out of my hands," Roxie answered, her eyes on the women in the kitchen to make sure none of them came out while she was on the phone. "Is everything alright there?"

"The same as always, Roxie. Fine and dandy. You don't have to worry about what's going on here. Everything is taken care of."

"That's so good to know. Thank you. I'll call you soon, alright? And I'm sorry to call so late," Roxie said, her eyes still on the women inside.

"Don't worry about it, really. You take care of yourself. Everything is fine here." The woman said and Roxie could hear the smile in her voice.

"I hope so. I'll call soon. Goodbye." Roxie hung up

once the other woman said goodbye and stared down at the phone.

Life was far more complicated than she'd ever dreamed it was back when all she worried about was which ballet school she would get into. Tears sparkled in her eyes again, but she batted them away with a fierce swipe of her hand. She didn't have time to be weak, to cry, or moan about how shitty her life had been.

She had a man to get back, a man that she was afraid she loved more than she could have thought possible. Getting him back was the most important thing in her life right now. She'd give her own if that's what it took to make it happen.

Standing up, Roxie put the phone in the back pocket of her jeans and went back inside. If she was lucky, this would be the last night she had to spend without Lincoln by her side.

DARK DESIRES

~ A billionaire dark romance series ~

Dark Desire

Dark Rules

Dark Secret

Dark Time

Dark Truth

BARRE TO BAR

~ A billionaire second chance series ~

Dancing With Lies

Dancing With Temptation

Dancing With Doubt

Dancing With Guilt

Dancing With Redemption

TWISTED INTENTION
~ A billionaire revenge romance series ~
Twisted Beauty
Twisted Love
Twisted Fate

Mafia's Obsession
~ A hot mafia romance series ~
Mafia's Dirty Secret
Mafia's Fake Bride
Mafia's Final Play

Screaming Demons
~ An MC romance series full of suspense ~
Rough Start
Rough Ride
Rough Choice
Rough Patch
Rough Return
Rough Road
Rough Trip
Rough Night
Rough Love

Standalone Contemporary Romance
Billionaire in Vegas
Billionaire Hunt

Billionaire's Game
Billionaire Retreat
Billionaire On Air
A Chance To Love
Somebody To Love
Not Mine To Love

Check out Summer's entire collection at
www.summercooper.com/books

ABOUT SUMMER COOPER

Thank you so much for reading. Without you, it wouldn't be possible for me to be a full-time author. I hope you enjoy reading my books as much as I do writing them.

Besides (obviously!) reading and writing, I also love cuddling my dogs, shouting at Alexa, being upside down (aka Yoga) and driving my family cray-cray!

Get in touch at
hello@summercooper.com
www.summercooper.com

facebook.com/summercooperauthor
instagram.com/summercooperauthor
goodreads.com/summercooper
bookbub.com/profile/summer-cooper